BEN FRANKLIN'S IN MY BATHROOM!

Also by Candace Fleming

FICTION

The Fabled Fourth Graders of Aesop Elementary School

The Fabled Fifth Graders of Aesop Elementary School

NONFICTION

Amelia Lost: The Life and Disappearance of Amelia Earhart

The Great and Only Barnum: The Tremendous, Stupendous Life of Showman P. T. Barnum

BEN FRANKLIN'S IN MY BATHROOM!

BY **CANDACE FLEMING**

WITH ILLUSTRATIONS BY MARK FEARING

schwartz & wade books · new york

Text copyright © 2017 by Hungry Bunny, Inc.
Jacket art and interior illustrations copyright © 2017 by Mark Fearing

SERIES TITLE: HISTORY PALS was published in the United States by Schwartz & Wade Books, an imprint of Random House Children's Books, a division of Penguin Random House LLC, New York.

Schwartz & Wade Books and the colophon are trademarks of Penguin Random House LLC.

Visit us on the Web! randomhousekids.com

Educators and librarians, for a variety of teaching tools, visit us at RHTeachersLibrarians.com

Library of Congress Cataloging-in-Publication Data is available upon request.
ISBN 978-1-101-93406-7 (hc) — ISBN 978-1-101-93407-4 (lib. bdg.) — ISBN 978-1-101-93408-1 (ebook)

The text of this book is set in Adobe Caslon.
The illustrations were rendered in pencil and digitally manipulated.
Book design by Rachael Cole

Printed in the United States of America
2 4 6 8 10 9 7 5 3 1
First Edition

To those "Sandblasters,"
Barb, Penny, and Steph —C.F.

For my dad, who taught me
to love history —M.F.

CHAPTER ONE

OLIVE LAY ON HER belly under the kitchen table. She flapped her imaginary tail. "I am the mermaid princess Aquamarina," she said in a singsongy voice. "I demand that you release me from this dungeon and return me to the sea . . . before I dry up."

I looked up from my book—another graphic novel, this one about pirates—and rolled my eyes. "Can't you just sit down like a normal person and eat your cereal?"

She pretended to flap her tail again. "We mermaids do not eat cereal, especially not Sprouts 'n' Stuff." She wrinkled her nose. "The sprouts taste like weeds, and the stuff tastes like dirt."

"You're crazy," I said. I turned back to my book. The panels showed Blackbeard's victims walking the plank. *Argh! Save us! Splash!* A ring of sharks circled below. I grinned. You have to love graphic novels. They're

so ... well ... *graphic*! I could really see all the gruesome details.

Olive crawled out from under the table. "I think I'll have cheesy doodles for breakfast," she declared in her regular voice.

I put down my book. "Oh, no you don't," I said.

"Oh, yes I do," she said. She stuck out her tongue and headed for the snack cabinet. "You're not the boss of me."

"I'm the big brother. You're only seven."

"So? You're only ten," Olive shot back.

"Almost eleven," I corrected her.

At that, Olive stuck her thumbs in her ears and waggled her fingers. "Nyah! Nyah! Nyah!"

I could feel angry words starting to pile up inside me. It was like having a belly full of bats flapping their wings and fighting to get out.

"Why do you always have to be such a bat . . . I mean, brat?" I said through clenched teeth. Then, in my best Mom voice, I added, "Why can't you just listen for once?"

Olive poked out her lower lip. "You're a meanie."

I knew I was being mean. And I hate being mean. But I couldn't help it. I just felt so full of bats. I sucked in air, tried to get calm. "Look," I finally said. "We have just three weeks of summer left. I don't want to waste them on a bunch of dumb baby-sister drama."

In response, she cried, "I can't hear you! I can't hear you!" Then she hopped up onto a kitchen chair. "Princess Aquamarina will now return to her watery world." She raised her hands in a diving position.

"Stop!" I grabbed at her.

Olive twisted away. "Do not touch the mermaid." She bumped against the table, sending her bowl of now-soggy Sprouts 'n' Stuff crashing to the floor.

"Hey!" called a sharp voice from upstairs. Mom came out of her attic studio and stood on the upstairs landing, peering down at us. She had a pencil stuck behind her ear and a worried look on her face. "I can hear you two all the way up here. What's the problem?"

I glared at Olive.

She hopped off the chair. Her hands dropped to her sides.

"There's no problem," I said.

"Nope, no problem," Olive said.

"It sounded like a problem," said Mom. Her voice was tired.

"We were just messing around," I said. "Sorry we got you out of your studio."

Our mom is the author-illustrator of the Bumble Bunnies series of children's books.

But after twenty-two bunny adventures, she was having trouble coming up with an idea for the twenty-third. And it was due to her publisher in less than a week.

"I'm blank," Mom had groaned just yesterday morning. She'd tugged on her hair, a sure sign she was feeling stressed. "Empty. Clean out of inspiration."

For the rest of the day, I had thought about my mom's "blankness" and how awful it must feel. I saw it in my mind all dark and echo-y like a cave, or a cellar, or my great-aunt Helen's bathroom. I guess that's what happens when you read as many graphic novels as I do. You start picturing all kinds of images in your head. Anyway, I thought maybe I could fix things.

So that night, I'd hopped to the supper table wearing a homemade Bumble Bunnies costume complete with floppy construction paper ears, a pink-painted nose, and a fluffy cotton-puff tail. It was so embarrassing I almost couldn't stand it. But after Dad left, I'd vowed to myself to help Mom any way I could . . . even if that meant going around dressed like a dumb bunny.

"Yeooow! A zombie kangaroo!" Olive had screamed when I appeared in the door-way. Then she put up her hands. "Don't eat

me, mate," she'd said in this ridiculous Australian accent before bursting into giggles.

I wanted to say that even a starving zombie wouldn't eat her tiny raisin brain, but I let it go.

By then, my mom was laughing, too.

But I wasn't. My costume wasn't

supposed to be funny. It was supposed to be inspirational. It was supposed to give Mom some confidence for Bumble Bunnies number twenty-three. Geez, if I'd wanted to be funny I would have put rubber vomit on their plates right next to the peas.

I guess my mom could see that my feelings were hurt. She came over and hugged me. "Oh, Nolan, my Mr. Fix-It," she said. "I know what you're trying to do, and it's really very sweet. Thank you, honey."

"Yeah, sure, Mom," I said, trying to act cool. But inside I'd felt terrible. It seemed like no matter how hard I tried, I couldn't make things right ... not the way Dad used to.

I was still feeling sort of bad about it this morning, which explains why I was watching my annoying little sister. I wanted Mom to have some peace and quiet. I thought maybe it would cure her "blankness."

You can see how great *that* worked out.

"Argh," Mom groaned. "I have to get back to it. Can you kids handle things without me today? Nolan is in charge."

Olive sniffed. "So the bunny gets to be boss?"

"I got it under control," I said, elbowing her in the ribs.

Mom looked down at us with laser eyes for a second. Then she nodded and disappeared back into her studio.

I turned to my sister. "You heard Mom."

"Hmph! I don't take orders from rabbits." She flounced back to the table. "Hey, who's going to clean up this mess?"

The doorbell rang.

"I'll get it!" Olive raced to the door and yanked it open.

A package wrapped in plain brown paper sat on the stoop.

CHAPTER TWO

"IT'S FOR YOU," **SAID** Olive, pointing to my name written in big block letters on the package's side.

"But . . ." I shook my head. "It's not my birthday or anything."

Stepping out onto the porch, I looked up and down the street. No sign of a mailman. No delivery truck speeding away either.

I turned back to the package. Other than my name and address, it was completely blank. No return address. No shipping labels. Not even a single stamp.

"Come on, already. Open it!" said Olive. She swooped it up and ran inside.

At the kitchen counter, I tore away the brown paper wrapping.

"It's a ... It's a ... Aw, it's just an old box," said Olive.

It was more like a case made of dark wood, and so pitted and scratched I was pretty sure it was some kind of antique. It had a hinged lid held shut by a brass latch. And engraved on its side in gold block letters were the words PROPERTY OF H.H.

"Who's H.H.?" asked Olive.

I shrugged. "The box's owner, I guess."

"So why'd it get sent to you?"

"It must be a mistake."

Olive grabbed at the box. "Let's see what's inside."

"Hold on a minute. Be careful."

Olive turned the latch. The front fell open to reveal . . .

"A bunch of junk," she said.

Built into the box were wires and coils and metal plates. In one corner was a dial printed with a weird combination of letters and numbers:

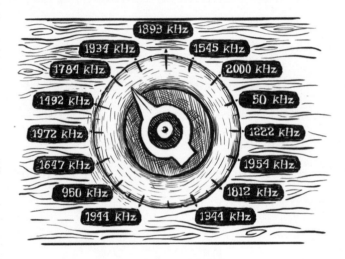

In another corner a shiny stone glinted in a tiny brass box. Above it, a wire no thicker than a cat's whisker hung from a miniature lever.

And in the middle, attached to a tiny post, sat a pair of old-fashioned headphones.

"What is it?" asked Olive.

I studied it. I'd seen something like it last year when my class had taken a field trip to our local history museum. "We learn from the past how to live in the present." That's what my teacher, Mr. Druff, had said. He'd even made us write it down in our social studies notebooks.

"It's a crystal radio set," I said now. "It was invented in the 1920s about the same time as bubble gum, the lie detector test, and frozen peas."

Mr. Druff's dumb history saying wasn't the only thing he'd made us write down that day.

Olive made a face. "That thing's a *radio*?"

"An old-timey one," I explained. "Before factories started making radios, people made their own. I guess it was a pretty simple thing to do. They could actually pick up broadcasts from faraway places like Paris and New York City."

Boy, would Mr. Druff be proud.

"Nerd," Olive said under her breath.

Then a part of my brain hesitated, told me to use caution. Who had sent this? And why to me? And why—

"So what are we waiting for?" Olive said. "Turn it on!"

"Hold up. I ... I don't know how this thing works. Or even *if* it works."

"There's only one way to find out," said Olive. She jiggled a few wires. "Testing, testing. This is Olive Veronica Stanberry. Testing, testing."

I snorted. "It's not a two-way radio, doofus. You don't talk to it. It talks to you."

"I know that," retorted Olive, although her suddenly pink cheeks told me she hadn't known. "I was just ... you know ... checking it out."

She took hold of the little lever, brushing the cat-whisker wire across the stone.

Nothing happened.

She did it again.

"Forget it. It doesn't work," I said.

"But I wanted to hear Paris," grumped Olive. *"Buenos dias, amigos!"*

"That's Spanish, not French," I corrected her.

"Whatever," she whined. "I still wanted to hear it." She poked out her lower lip and stomped her feet so loud we almost didn't notice that the stone had started glinting.

"I think it's alive, Nolan," she said.

I shook my head. "It's probably just a reflection or something." What other explanation was there?

Olive reached out and brushed the cat whisker over the stone a third time.

It glowed brighter. Whiter. Crystal white.

"It's working!" cried Olive.

My heart started beating faster. Squinting into the light, I looked at the radio from every angle. There didn't seem to be anything unusual about it . . . except that glowing stone.

From the headphones came an electrical hum.

"Quick, put them on," said Olive.

My hand hovered over them. Part of me didn't want to do it. I had this strange feeling that I was standing on a cliff, about to jump into . . . What? *It's just a junky old crystal radio,* I told myself. *What could be dangerous about that?*

I fit the headphones over my ears.

"Do you hear anything?" demanded Olive. "Do you?"

I shook my head.

She turned the dial a click. "How about now?"

Khhhhh!

"Static," I said.

She turned it another click.

Khhhhh!

She turned it a third click.

Khhhhh . . .

Then a voice.

Faint. Tinny. Punctuated by static: "Early to bed . . . *khhhhh* . . . early to rise . . . *khhhhh* . . . Haste makes . . . *khhhhh* . . ."

"What's going on? Can you hear anything? Let me try." She snatched at the headphones.

Suddenly, chairs, tables, walls, ceilings, *everything* blurred and fell out of focus, hard edges dissolving into nothingness. I looked at Olive. Only she and I appeared to remain solid.

"What's happening?" she cried.

I reached out for her. Tried to grab her. Missed.

My stomach lurched. For one second I got that feeling you get when you watch a 3-D movie without the glasses. Off-kilter. Out of whack. There was a loud *POP!* like a gazillion soap bubbles all bursting at once.

Then the room snapped back into focus.

The feeling passed.

And Olive screamed.

I whirled.

In the doorway between the kitchen and

family room stood a short, round-faced man. He wore a brown coat and knee-length silk pants, and his fringe of long, graying hair was tied back with a ribbon. Squarish little glasses perched on his nose. An odd-shaped fur cap sat crooked on his head. Looking around with a dazed expression, he reeled slightly and gripped the back of a kitchen chair for support.

I blinked

I blinked again.

Olive pointed, unable to speak.

"You're . . . you're . . . ," I finally blurted out. "You're . . . B-B . . . Benjamin Franklin!"

CHAPTER THREE

"DO MY SENSES DECEIVE me?" Benjamin Franklin muttered to himself. "Zoons, but I must be dreaming." He pinched himself. "Wake thee up, Ben."

He slapped his cheeks. "Rouse thyself."

He shook his head. "I am most assuredly awake."

Lifting his fur cap, he scratched his head like it would help him think. "Could this all be a hallucination brought on by bad ale, or bilious fever, or . . ." He snapped his fingers. "Steak and kidney pie! Oh, but I should never have eaten it all. A full belly makes a dull brain."

He was so busy pondering that he didn't seem to notice Olive and me standing there.

That is, until Olive stepped up and poked him in the tummy. "You aren't really Benjamin Franklin, are you?"

He jumped, startled, and stared at my sister before drawing himself up. "Young lady, there are three things extremely hard: steel, a diamond, and to know one's self. Yet even in my discombobulated state, I can assure you that I am unquestionably Benjamin Franklin."

"Okey-dokey," said Olive. She turned to me. "He's real."

"None of this can be real," I said. "You must be a hallucination."

"It is scientifically impossible for all three of us to be experiencing the same hallucination," he replied.

I shook my head. There had to be some explanation for what was happening. There just had to be. "I know," I finally said. "You're a ghost."

He pinched himself again. "As you can see, I am most decidedly flesh and bone."

Olive's eyes sparkled. "We brought back

Benjamin Franklin! With that radio thingy. We really, truly brought him back!"

I glanced over at the crystal radio. It wasn't glowing or chattering anymore. It just sat there on the counter, dark and silent.

"That's not possible." But even as I said the words, I knew it was. Somehow, some way, we had turned the dial, and instead of modern-day Paris or New York City, we'd tuned in to colonial America. I shook my head again. "This is crazy."

"But so cool," said Olive.

"Ahem!" Benjamin Franklin coughed to get our attention. "It appears you children know who I am, and yet I do not know you, or for that matter where I am."

Olive nudged me forward. "You tell him."

I made a face at her. Then I turned to Benjamin Franklin. I couldn't believe what I was about to say. "Um … hiya. I mean, greetings, Mr. Franklin, sir. I'm ... er ... Nolan Stanberry, and that's my sister ..."

"Olive." She waggled her fingers and gave him a gap-toothed smile.

Pulling off his fur cap, he took a little bow. "I am charmed to make your acquaintance."

"Us too ... um ... I ... Charmed, that is," I said. I took a deep breath, knowing what I had to say. "Mr. Franklin ..."

"Call me Ben. Everyone does."

I tried again. "Ben, you might want to sit down for this."

"For what?"

It was time to break the news. "You're not in Philadelphia anymore."

He raised an eyebrow.

"You're in Rolling Hills, Illinois. In twenty-first-century America."

I could see my words sinking in by the changing expression on his face.

Disbelief: "This cannot be. It breaks with all known scientific principles."

Surprise: "And yet, the scientific mind is ever questioning. . . ."

Wonder: "Does the lad speak true?
Have I traveled across two centuries?"

Excitement: "I have! I truly have!"

"I think he took that pretty well," I said to Olive.

"Oh, yeah," she replied.

Ben spun in an excited circle, giggling and holding his head as if it might burst. Finally, he paused, and looked over at Olive and me. "I beg you children, pray show me more of your century's innovations and advancements before I return to my own. I shan't waste this precious opportunity."

He looked around the kitchen and pointed to an object on the counter. "Tell me. What is that device?"

"It's a toaster," said Olive. "You plug it in, and the bread toasts."

"The coils heat by electricity," I added.

Ben gasped. "Did you say electricity? Could it be that my modest experiment with kite and key has come to something?"

Olive grinned and flipped the wall switch. The light above the kitchen table snapped on.

Ben gazed up at it. "Oh, it does work. It works!" He nodded toward the switch. "May I?"

"Sure," said Olive.

Ben snapped the light off. Then on. Then off. Then on again.

"Zoons, but it works every time!" He rubbed his hands together. "I must see more."

I pulled Olive aside. "I think he's seen enough," I whispered. I glanced up the stairs, expecting Mom to appear at any moment. This would *definitely* not make things easier for her. Or us. "Ben has to go back right now, like this very instant. Before anyone finds out he's been here." I glanced over at the radio. "It should be pretty easy. Just a few clicks of the dial and—"

"Hey, Ben, look at *this*!" cried Olive. Ignoring me, she flipped a switch on the blender.

VROOM!

"And *this*!" She pushed the buttons on the microwave.

BEEP-BEEP!

"And *this*!" She turned on the coffee grinder.

GRRRRR!

"No, stop!" I called to her. "Didn't you hear what I said?"

But she and Ben were off—pushing buttons, pulling levers, flipping switches, plugging in cords and . . .

Foosh!

. . . flushing the toilet in the guest bathroom. I could see them through the open doorway, Ben bent over in deep concentration.

"By Jove, a self-cleaning commode," he declared. "Ingenious."

He flushed again.

Foosh!

"Where does the clean water come from?"

Foosh!

"Where does the dirty water go?"

Foosh!

"The scientific mind is ever questioning!"

"What's all that flushing?" Mom called from the top of the stairs. "Is someone sick?"

Olive rushed out into the hallway.

I rushed after her.

"Don't worry, Mom," Olive called back. "It's just Ben Franklin experimenting with—"

I slapped my hand over Olive's big mouth.

"Too much juice," I shouted up the stairs. "I drank too much juice."

There was a long silence.

I could tell Mom was standing there, deciding whether she should come down. "Are you sure everything's under control, Nolan?"

"Sure, I'm sure," I said. I shook my head. Mothers, geez. What goes on in their brains? They get all suspicious over a little toilet flushing. But bunches of appliances zapping on and off? *That* doesn't faze them one bit.

Foosh!

Mom sighed and shut her door.

Olive squirmed away. She wiped her lips. "Lemme go!"

I could feel things hurtling out of control. "He *has* to go back. *Now.*"

From the laundry room came the sound of the dryer buzzing.

"Incredible!" said Ben.

"Why?" asked Olive. "He's our new friend—our really, really, really *old* new friend."

The ceiling fan in the family room whirred.

"Stupendous!"

"I want to keep him," said Olive.

"Are you kidding? He's Ben Franklin, not a goldfish."

The television blared.

"Zoons, but it boggles the mind!" Ben sat

down, mesmerized by the flashing images. "What is this marvel?"

Olive glanced in through the doorway. "Oh, that's a reality show called *Real or Wig*. The guest stars try to figure out if the person's hair is really their own, or—"

"Olive!" I yelled, but then caught myself and whispered through gritted teeth, "Olive!"

She looked at me.

"This is serious," I said. "He can't stay."

"Wig!" Ben shouted at the television.

She looked back at the television, giggled, and made a buzzer sound. "*Errrrrnt!* Sorry, that's just a super-bad haircut. It's called a mullet."

I grabbed her arm. "Listen, will you? Sure, it would be fun to keep Ben around. It'd probably be the coolest thing ever. But that radio, or whatever it is—"

"It's a time machine." She rolled her eyes. "Obviously."

"All I'm saying is that we have to keep it—and *him*—secret. We can't let anyone know. Not even Mom."

"Why not?"

I couldn't explain. I just knew deep down in my guts that we needed to keep all this quiet.

"Wig!" shouted Ben again.

I walked into the family room and flipped off the Reality Channel.

Ben looked disappointed.

Olive harrumphed. "All right, fine, we'll send him back. . . ."

I sighed with relief.

"Right *after* the tea party."

Oh, brother.

CHAPTER FOUR

BEN FRANKLIN SURE COULD eat. Besides a whole box of pizza puffs, he inhaled half a bag of potato chips, two peanut butter and strawberry jam sandwiches, a stack of marshmallow cookies, and three teacups of tropical fruit punch, which he gulped down with his pinky raised. He wouldn't touch the Sprouts 'n' Stuff, though, not after he'd sampled a bite.

"They taste," he said, "like weeds and dirt."

Olive shot me a look. "Told you so." She held out a bag to Ben. "Would you care for a

few more cheesy doodles?" she said in her best tea party voice.

"Waste not, want not," said Ben.

She shook out the last of the doodles onto his Princess Aquamarina tea party plate.

He crunched on one. "Ah, delicious doo-doo."

Olive giggled. "Not doo-doo, silly. *Doodles.* A doo-doo is—"

I thumped the crystal radio onto the kitchen table.

Ben's eyes lit up. "What, pray tell, is that?"

"It think it's how you got here," I explained. "And how we'll be able to send you back." I picked up the headphones.

"Not yet!" cried Olive. She snatched the headphones away. "I want Ben to tell me a story first."

"No, Olive. We have to send him home."

She stuck out her chin.

"Come on," I said. "Give them."

"Ben's traveled here from a long time ago, and I want to know what it was like back then." She turned to Ben. "Tell us a story from colonial days. Pretty please?"

I groaned. "We don't have time for this. Mom could come downstairs any second."

"Just one," she said.

Ben broke in. "At the risk of sounding immodest, I am a renowned raconteur. My storytelling abilities are exemplary."

"See? He's exempt ... expat ... He's good!" insisted Olive.

Geez, she was stubborn. I raised my hands in defeat.

"Hooray!" whooped my sister. She wiggled around, getting comfortable in her chair.

"But just one," I added firmly.

Ben nodded. "I confess, sitting here in this electrified room with these unusual yet delicious comestibles *does* put me in mind of a story."

He started to talk. And as he did, I could see the pictures in my mind's eye. All the details. Just like in a graphic novel.

Olive clapped. "You *are* a good storyteller."

"Thank you, young Olive."

"I'm glad you didn't tell that kite-in-the-thunderstorm story," I said. "I've heard that one a gazillion times. But this one was all new to me."

Ben raised an eyebrow. "You have heard tell of my kite experiment?"

"Everyone's heard that," said Olive.

I nodded. "It's a pretty famous story from American history, what my teacher, Mr. Druff, calls a greatest hit. Our social studies book at school was full of your greatest hits."

At that, Ben's chest puffed up like a peacock's. "Tell me, which of my other . . . er . . . greatest hits have made it into your history books?"

I thought a moment. "The Franklin stove," I said. "The lightning rod. The public library."

"Rolling Hills has a library," interjected Olive.

"Every town does," I added.

Ben's chest swelled so big I thought the brass buttons on his coat were going to pop right off. "I also had the idea of forming clubs of active men to combat Philadelphia's fires."

"Fire departments," I said.

"Every town has one of those, too," said Olive.

"Oh, but I am reeling with joy!" said Ben.

Olive bounced up and down in her chair.

"Let's show him. Come on, Nolan, let's take Ben to the library."

Ben bounced too. "That is a splendid idea. You are a precocious young lady, Miss Olive."

"No, it is not a splendid idea," I said. I turned to my sister. "You can't walk around town with Benjamin Franklin. He's the real guy . . . you know, Founding Father, inventor of electricity, wearer of fur cap and short pants. From the past. Famous dead guy."

"Nolan!" exclaimed Olive. "Don't call him that. . . ."

"Many pardons for interrupting your discussion," Ben cut in, "but I believe there is something unusual happening at yonder window."

I turned.

The glassy eye of a periscope peeked just above the sill.

CHAPTER FIVE

I SLIPPED OUT THE back door and raced around the side of the house.

A kid wearing a trench coat kneeled in the bushes beneath our kitchen window. I couldn't see his face because it was pressed against the eyepiece of a handheld periscope. But I knew who it was. Only one kid in Rolling Hills owned a trench coat.

"Tommy Tuttle," I said.

Still on his knees, Tommy lowered the periscope and turned to look at me. Calmly, as if hiding in bushes were as normal as

crossing the street, he stood and wiped the dirt off his knees. Then he stepped out from behind the shrubbery. "Hello there, Nolan," he said, all fake friendly and even fakier innocent. "I just stopped by for a snoop . . . I mean, a *scoop* of sugar." He went on. "I'm baking brownie bites. I'm famous for my brownie bites."

I like Tommy about as much as I like Grandma's broccoli-and-onion casserole.

Mostly I try to stay away from him. But when a kid is in your grade *and* lives on your block, it's kind of impossible.

"I see you've got an unusual visitor," he said. "Who is he, huh? You can tell me."

I narrowed my eyes. "What's it to you?"

"Just curious." Tommy smirked. "Is that

your grandpa in there? He looks really old. He dresses funny too."

"You should talk," I replied, glaring.

"Hmmm . . . who does he remind me of?"
Tommy pretended to think a second; then
he snapped his fingers. "I know! Benjamin
Franklin. Yeah, your grandpa reminds me of
Benjamin Franklin."

I could feel my belly filling with bats
again. "Get out of my bushes!" I hollered.

Tommy raised his hands. "Oh, gee, Nolan,
I didn't mean to make you mad. But it *is*
curious how much that geezer in your house

resembles good old Ben. He looks just like the guy on the hundred-dollar bill. Weird that's he's so interested in toasters. And blenders. And overhead lights."

"How long have you been out here snooping, huh?" I demanded.

"Since I saw that strange package on—"

"No, don't bother," I interrupted. "Just get lost."

"Aren't *you* touchy," he said, sneering. "And you know who's touchy? People who have something to hide."

I tried to laugh, but my mouth had gone dry and I could only cough. What else had Tommy seen through his periscope?

"You might as well confess," Tommy went on. "No secret is safe when I'm on the case."

That's what I was afraid of. Tommy *would* snoop out the truth. And he *would* broadcast it all over town.

"Come on, Nolan. Spill it," he pressed.

The bats in my gut were going nuts. Struggling to keep cool, I tightened my fists. "I mean it, Tommy. Take your periscope and get out of here."

He shrugged. "Have it your way. But I *will* find out what's going on."

After Tommy left, I stood there in the bushes letting the bats fly off. This was all too much. Tommy Tuttle. That crazy crystal radio. Ben Franklin in my kitchen! I hurried inside. Ben had to go back to the time of powdered wigs and buckled shoes. Right *now*.

The kitchen was empty.

So was the family room.

And the guest bathroom.

"Olive?" I called.

That's when I saw the note on the kitchen counter. With a feather plucked from my mother's centerpiece and dipped into a cup of chocolate pudding, Ben had written with lots of flourishes:

Master Nolan—
Young Olive and I have
ventured out to see the sights
of this remarkable century.
Not wishing to squander
time, for that's the stuff life
is made of, we chose not to
wait for your return. We
would, however, be delighted
if you joined us. We intend to
visit your public library first.
I am, as always—

B. Franklin

Through gritted teeth, I muttered, "I'm going to kill her."

CHAPTER SIX

ROLLING HILLS IS A small town, so it didn't take long for me to get to the public library—a two-story building made of limestone. It has tall white columns and a wide porch that goes across the whole front. Some millionaire named Andrew Carnegie donated the building to the town more than a hundred years ago, which explains why it's called the Rolling Hills Carnegie Public Library. It also explains why the place looks like something you might see on TV. You almost expect to see a couple of old people sitting outside in rocking chairs, talking about the good old days.

I spotted Olive and Ben standing on the front steps. A small crowd had gathered around them.

"How come you're wearing your Halloween costume?" asked a little girl in a tiger-striped tutu and purple polka-dot rain boots. She giggled. "You look silly."

"Come on, buddy," said Mr. Middleton, one of the tellers at my mom's bank. "Tell us who you're supposed to be."

"Are you trying to be Thomas Jefferson?" asked Tutu Girl's mother.

"He's Thomas Jefferson!" squealed Tutu Girl.

"Oh, no, no, Tom is much taller than I," replied Ben. He bowed. "I am Benjamin Franklin."

"I should have known by the glasses," Tutu Girl's mother said.

"Bifocals," said Ben. "I invented them."

"Oh, there you are!" cried Mrs. Bustamante, the library director. She weaved her way through the crowd, dodging and ducking and moving pretty good for a lady who's probably already in her thirties. She inspected Ben, growing slightly confused. "Benjamin Franklin? We were expecting Thomas Jefferson."

"Told ya!" Tutu Girl said.

Mrs. Bustamante grabbed Ben's arm, shook her head, and said, "Well, you'll just have to do. We have a room full of people waiting. Do you know *anything* about Jefferson?"

"Indeed, I do, madam," Ben said as she swept him along.

"And why are you wearing a squirrel?" she asked.

"It's marten fur, madam. I bought it from a most fashionable Philadelphia hatmaker," replied Ben.

"Looks like squirrel to me," insisted Mrs. Bustamante. "Now, let's get you inside and set up."

"Set up?" asked Olive.

Mrs. Bustamante didn't answer. She bustled them into the library.

I took the stairs two at a time, barreling after them into the lobby.

The guy behind the checkout desk stood. He didn't say a word. He just glared at me and made a circling motion with one beefy finger. He pointed at the door I'd just come in.

"Huh?"

Still wordless, he kept pointing. Boy, he really took "quiet in the library" to a whole new level.

Finally, I got it. "Oh," I said. I backed out the door, then *walked* in. "Better?"

He just glared.

By this time, Ben and Olive were nowhere in sight. I turned in a complete circle, scanning the place—the adult department, the reference desk, the kids' section where the graphic novels were shelved. I wondered briefly if the library had gotten any new titles . . . then quickly came to my senses. I looked over at the checkout guy. "Did a little girl with frizzy red hair come by here with Ben Fra— I mean, a guy who looks like Ben Franklin?"

He pointed down the hall toward the meeting room.

I *walked* down the hall and pushed open the door.

The room was packed with people sitting on folding chairs. At the front Mrs.

Bustamante stood beside Ben. Behind them hung a banner that read:

The Rolling Hills Carnegie Public Library presents HEROES FROM HISTORY Meet Thomas Jefferson

I stood there, confused. What was going on? Then it hit me: Mrs. Bustamante and the others thought Ben was an impersonator. The wrong one, but still a Founding Father. And they expected him to give a program.

"Nolan! Hey, Nolan!" Olive waved at me from the second row, using a couple of library flyers as if they were pom-poms. She patted the empty chair next to her. "This is fun, isn't it? Ben's going to put on a show."

I sat down next to her. "No, this is not fun," I groaned. "This is definitely not fun."

Mrs. Bustamante twirled up to the microphone. "Thank you all for coming to yet another presentation in our ongoing American history series. In past weeks we've met the first female pilot to fly across the Atlantic and the homespun president who ended slavery. Today we make another historical acquaintance. Perhaps not the one we'd hoped for, but ... well ... without further ado, ladies and gentlemen ..." She extended her arm toward Ben. "Meet Ben Franklin."

The audience clapped.

Mrs. Bustamante nudged him toward the podium.

And Ben swept off his hat. "I confess I had not expected to address such a learned meeting when I arrived in the twenty-first century."

The audience laughed. If only they knew it wasn't a joke.

"Books and libraries are marvelous things," continued Ben. "It is like I always say, reading makes a full man."

"Abraham Lincoln said exactly the same thing last week," a woman in the first row piped up.

"Abraham *who*?" said Ben. He shrugged. "Whoever he is, he stole that saying from me."

The audience laughed again.

Olive jumped to her feet. "How about another story, Ben? About colonial days."

The grown-ups around us smiled. It was like they actually thought my bigmouthed sister was cute or something.

Ben looked around the room. "It seems," he said, smiling, "that I have a story suitable for this very occasion."

And once again, as he talked, my mind filled with pictures.

Books were scarce in Philadelphia.

Newspapers. Ballads. Almanacs. All these could be purchased in the city. But there was not a single bookseller.

Those who loved reading had to get their books from England.

This was so expensive that I could only afford a book or two a year.

But I had an idea to change all that.

This is my men's club. We call ourselves the Junto, and we are a group of inquirers. Every Friday evening, we meet to talk of sunrays, waterspouts, musical instruments, and more.

Above all, we talk of books.

Always books.

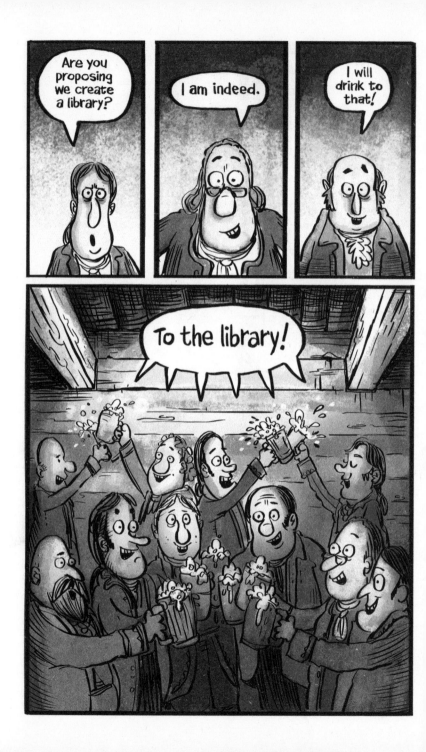

Before long our public library contained three hundred books.

Reading became quite fashionable in Philadelphia. And travelers to our fair city noticed that we were smarter and better informed than citizens of other cities.

Of course, a good idea is bound to be copied. Public libraries, like Englishmen, soon flourished in the American colonies.

New York

South Carolina

Massachusetts

I swear, Ben's stories were almost as good as *The Pirate's Blood.* The audience must have thought so too. They clapped and whistled like crazy.

"I'd almost believe it was Ben himself," gushed the first-row woman to the man sitting beside her.

The man grumbled. "He's too thin. And that hat makes him look like he's wearing a squirrel."

Mrs. Bustamante nodded in agreement.

I sat up taller in my seat. Maybe our secret was safe after all.

The door banged open. A man wearing a white wig, short pants, and a pair of loafers with fake buckles glued to them rushed in. "Sorry I'm late," he panted. "I got caught in traffic."

Mrs. Bustamante did a double take.

So did the audience.

So did both Founding Fathers.

"Who's that guy?" asked Olive.

"Mr. Jefferson!" Mrs. Bustamante exclaimed.

I slid back down in my seat.

Thomas Jefferson pointed an accusing finger at Ben. "Hey, this is *my* gig. That guy's a poser!"

Ben raised his eyebrows. "Good sir, I am standing, not posing."

Jefferson took out a piece of paper and

handed it to the library director. "Proof that I am who I say I am."

Mrs. Bustamante scanned the paper. "This is the talent agency's contract. But if you are you, who"—she turned to Ben—"are you?"

"An imposter impersonator!" cried Jefferson. "And a sad imitation. Just look at that costume. It's all wrong!"

At the podium, Ben's mouth quirked up at the corners, and his eyes twinkled. He sounded on the verge of giggling when he asked, "And what, sir, might be improper about my . . . *costume?*"

"The stockings. The jacket. That ridiculous beaver hat."

"I thought it was squirrel," said Mrs. Bustamante.

"Marten," Ben corrected her. "It is marten fur."

Jefferson snorted. "Benjamin Franklin never owned a marten fur hat in his life.

You evidently know nothing about that great man."

Ben stepped out from behind the podium. "You have convinced me, Tom, that you have a superior grasp of colonial America. Therefore, I concede the floor to you."

The audience buzzed as Ben sat down on the other side of me. "I shall listen from here with rapt attention."

"Yes ... well ... good," said Jefferson with a sniff.

"After all, it is ill manners to silence a fool," added Ben under his breath. He crossed his arms over his chest, ready to listen.

Jefferson pulled a stack of note cards from his breeches pocket. He cleared his throat. "We hold these truths to be self-evident," he began.

"We should really go," I whispered to Ben. Now seemed like our best chance to slip away. Mrs. Bustamante couldn't yell at us, or call the police, in front of a room full of people.

We stood.

But just then, Mrs. Bustamante stepped up to the microphone. "I'm so sorry, Mr. Jefferson, but we're out of time."

"Wait . . . I . . . ," stammered Jefferson.

She continued. "Still, I hope you'll all return next week to meet John Adams."

"I already have," said Ben.

"Now I invite everyone to join us for lemonade and cookies in the youth service department," she concluded.

Her announcement cleared the room out pretty quick.

"Come on," I urged.

"But cookies!" said Olive.

Oh, brother.

I hustled them both past the glaring man at the front desk, out the door, and down the stairs.

I didn't relax until we reached the sidewalk.

"Not so fast, you three," shouted Mrs. Bustamante. She rushed down the stairs after us.

"I think we should run now," suggested Olive.

But the librarian was smiling. "I just wanted to say thank you to, er ... Mr. Franklin." She turned to him. "You were marvelous. Absolutely marvelous."

Ben bowed his thanks.

She pulled Olive and me aside. "How long has your grandfather been like this?" she asked, her eyes full of sympathy.

Ben overheard her. "About three hundred years," he replied.

And with that, we left Mrs. Bustamante standing there, her mouth opening and shutting.

CHAPTER SEVEN

WE HEADED TOWARD HOME, Ben poking his nose everywhere like a hound dog on a scent.

Cars. Bicycles. Sprinklers. Stoplights. Parking meters. Skateboards. Basketball hoops. Streetlamps. Trash cans. Motorcycles. Street signs. Lawn mowers. A fire hydrant. A Labradoodle sniffing the fire hydrant. Swing sets. Barbecue grills. Bermuda grass.

Across Tremont Street, two girls pointed at him and laughed. A passing car slowed and honked. A man carrying a grocery bag stared.

"Can we hurry it along?" I asked.

"Haste makes waste," said Ben.

We turned the corner. Rolling Hills Elementary came into view.

"Is this where you attend school, lad?" asked Ben.

"We both go here," Olive butted in. "I'm going into second grade."

"You *both* go? Boys *and* girls? *Together?*" Ben raised his eyebrows. "In my day, only boys attend school. Girls are taught at home."

Olive made a face. "That stinks."

"I am curious," Ben went on. "Do boys and girls learn the same subjects? Latin, geography, diction?"

"Math, science, reading," I said. "Social studies . . ."

"Swimming," added Olive.

"That's day camp, not school," I corrected her.

"So what? I'm learning it, aren't I?" She turned to Ben. "Someday I'm going to be as good a swimmer as mermaid princess Aquamarina."

"Swimming lessons!" exclaimed Ben. "Imagine that."

We crossed Kenton Avenue.

"I have long advocated the benefits of swimming," Ben went on, "although, back home, the activity is considered dangerous and unsanitary. Few people know how to swim. But I love it. I once even considered starting my own swimming school."

"You swim?" I asked. Ben didn't exactly look like an athlete.

"Miles at a time," he replied. "I taught myself as a boy from a book called *The Art of Swimming*. Besides the basic strokes, I learned a number of tricks." He smiled. "And I invented a few of my own."

As he continued to talk, pictures started popping into my mind.

My father made and sold soap and candles on Hanover Street in the city of Boston.

I too worked at the shop.

They worked . . .

for a while. My wrists grew sore and my arms ached.

What I needed was *two* pairs of paddles.

SPLASH!

They worked...

for a while. But soon my wrists *and* ankles ached.

If not entirely successful, the experiment had been made.

And I had learned that my invention — let us call them swim fins — *did* increase speed, if rather uncomfortably.

"You know what we should do?" cried
Olive when Ben finished.

Oh geez, uh-uh, no way. She better not
say it.

"Let's go swimming!"

She said it.

And then she took off down the sidewalk.

CHAPTER EIGHT

THE THREE OF US stood outside the tall fence that surrounded the community pool. From the other side came the sounds of splashing and laughter and the sharp *tweeeeet* of the lifeguards' whistles.

Ben peeked over the chain links. "A pond

made especially for swimming. What an extraordinary idea!" he exclaimed.

"It's called a swimming pool," said Olive.

"We are *not* going in," I said. "We are absolutely not swimming."

"Why not?" asked Olive.

I pointed at Ben. "Time travel? Return trip? Famous dead guy? Does any of that ring a bell?"

"But I want to swim with B-e-e-e-n," she whined.

I tried a different argument. "You're not wearing a bathing suit."

"Sure I am. See?" Olive lifted her T-shirt to reveal her sparkly purple one-piece underneath. "Mermaids always wear their bathing suits."

"What a coincidence," said Ben. "So do I. During hot summer months I prefer to don my bathing garment rather than underclothes. One never knows, after all, when one may be struck with the urge to strip off one's clothing and plunge into the water."

Olive nodded. "I know, right?"

"One must be prepared for every opportunity," said Ben.

"Totally," agreed Olive.

Oh, brother.

Olive went around to the entrance. We followed.

The bored teenager at the front desk

didn't bother to look up from her phone. "Pass?"

"Right here," said Olive. She pulled it out of her back pocket. "Olive and Nolan Stanberry . . . and one guest."

I guess mermaids always carry their pool passes too.

Still ogling her phone, the teenager waved us in.

"Meet you on the other side," said Olive as she headed into the girls' locker room.

Ben and I went into the boys'.

Maybe, I hoped, without his goofy colonial clothes, no one would recognize him. Maybe he'd look like any other old guy in a bathing suit.

"Oh, this is a jolly lark," said Ben as he kicked off his buckled shoes and peeled off his knee-high stockings.

I wrinkled my nose. Here's a fact you won't find in the history books: Benjamin Franklin had stinky feet.

Oh, and knobby knees.

He stripped down to his "bathing garment."

My mouth fell open.

His trunks, if you could call them that, had flowers on them. Big red flowers. And that wasn't the worst part. They reached to his knees, and were trimmed in . . . *lace.* Inch-wide, ruffly lace. It made his suit look like a pair of ladies' long underwear.

Ben saw me staring. "My wife, Deborah, sewed this to my exact specifications," he said, patting his potbelly. "I am pleased to say it is waterproof and seam-tight."

"Boy, am I glad to hear that," I said.

We padded out to the pool area. Everyone was there. And when I say everyone, I mean *everyone*. About a million kids from school were splashing, diving, and floating around on inflatable rings. Brian Golladay and a couple of other guys from my class were goofing around by the showers, snapping towels at one another and basically acting like dorks. When they saw Ben they stopped. One of the guys pointed. They all started laughing.

"Hey, Stanberry!" C. J. McCabe called from the concession line. "What's the matter? You forget to wear your tablecloth?"

The two girls standing behind him started to giggle.

"This is all your fault," I said to Olive, who had emerged from the locker room.

"They're just meanies." She dropped her pile of clothes next to Ben's on a lounge chair.

All eyes were on Ben as he and Olive headed for the water.

Oblivious to the pointing and staring, he stood at the pool's edge. He did a series of knee bends. Down, then up, down, then up, with great big gusts of breath and lots of

creaking joints. "For the blood, Nolan," he shouted to where I sat hunched on the lounge chair. "And for the muscles."

I could feel my reputation plunging toward geekdom with every knee bend.

Behind me the guys snickered.

Next Ben windmilled his arms above his head. Then he flapped them behind his back and in front of his belly.

"It's a bird. . . . It's a plane. . . . It's Bloomer Man!" hooted C.J.

The girls giggled again.

Ben waded into the deep water and dove.

From where I sat, all I could see were the bobbing heads and flapping arms of the other swimmers, then—

"Ahhhhh!"

Ben burst from the water like a dolphin. He streaked up . . . up . . . up . . . until almost all of his body was out of the water. For a

single second he seemed to hang there, before curving gracefully to his right and slipping back below the surface without even the tiniest splash.

"Oooh, he's a mermaid," squealed Olive.

"Whoa!" cried C.J. "Did you see that?"

Kids began moving away from the center of the pool, giving Ben room.

A moment later, his legs rose out of the water. Just his legs. They scissored, toes pointed. Then they disappeared to be replaced by Ben's head and chest. He spiraled, his arms held gracefully above his head.

Everyone moved to the sides of the pool to watch. It was like a scene from one of those old black-and-white movies where some couple starts whirling all around the dance floor, and everyone else clears out of the way to stare and cheer.

With the pool to himself, Ben went crazy. He did upside-down splits and cork-screw twists. He spun on his back in tight circles and did leg lifts, backward rolls, handstands, and somersaults. Finally, he swam over to where Olive sat with her feet dangling in the water.

"Is that mermaid swimming?" asked Olive.

"Stunt swimming," said Ben. "It is quite invigorating. And exceedingly healthful. In just minutes one can work all one's muscles."

"Will you teach me?" asked Olive.

"It would be my pleasure," said Ben.

"And me?" asked David Nichols, who was sitting next to her.

"And me too?" asked his friend Jeter Smolensky.

"The more the merrier," said Ben.

They gathered in the shallow end of the pool.

"We shall begin by learning to scull and flutter," said Ben.

Within minutes, he had them spinning on their backs while floating.

"I wanna learn *that*," cried C.J.

He jumped in and joined Ben's group.

So did Brian and the other guys from my class, as well as the girls from the concession stand and the two lifeguards.

Even a group of grown-ups got off their towels and waded in. This was sort of amazing, considering most parents only came to the pool to chat with other parents and catch up on their reading. Until that day, I'd never seen one put more than his or her foot in the pool. But now there they were, learning to scull and flutter, spiral and scissor.

Soon both kids and grown-ups were floating in circle formations. Spreading their arms wide, they held one another's hands,

then stuck their left legs in the circle's middle so their toes touched. On Ben's count, they gracefully lifted their legs into the air.

"Like a blossoming flower," instructed Ben. "That's it. Lovely, lovely!"

Next, they rested their left ears against their left shoulders and glided all together to their left. They switched, and glided all together to their right. They switched again . . . left. They switched again . . . right.

"By Poseidon's blessing, this is enchanting indeed!" cried Ben.

They rose and dove. They learned pinwheels, paddle kicks, pliés, and flips.

"Cross your ankles thusly," coached Ben. "Swivel your torsos."

Arms and legs waved. Tummies and torsos waggled. It looked like some crazy kind of water ballet.

Suddenly, Ben dove. Seconds later he rose from the water, slowly and dramatically. Above his head he held a grinning Olive.

"All hail Princess Aquamarina!" she squealed. Then she leaped, spun, and splashed back into the water.

Ben laughed and clapped. "Bravo, young Olive!"

Seeing them together made me think about all the fun Dad and I used to have. Maybe not swimming, but other stuff, like shooting baskets in the driveway and go-karting at Speed Zone.

"Hey, Nolan, did you see me?" cried Olive. She swam over to the edge near my lounge chair. "Did you see me be a mermaid? I'm a real mermaid!"

I wanted to be happy for her, but the bats were back. I scowled. "Yeah, I saw. So what?"

"Oooh, meet Mr. Crabby Pants," she drawled. "You should jump in, Nolan. Every ocean needs crabs."

"You're hilarious." I looked around. "Where's Ben? I want to get out of here."

Olive pointed.

The lesson had broken up, and Ben was out of the pool. But he was still hanging around a couple of moms who were complimenting him on his "teaching abilities" and his "charming way with the children."

Mrs. Delacruz wrapped a towel around his dripping shoulders. "We wouldn't want you to catch cold, now, would we?"

Another lady pecked him on the cheek. "You are a dear, sweet man."

"Oooh la la," squealed Olive. Then she started chanting, "Ben and some mothers swimming in the sea. *K-I-S-S-I-N-G*."

"Cut it out," I grumbled.

Ben didn't seem to mind, though. In-

stead, he kissed each of their hands. "Adieu, dear ladies."

Smooch!

Smooch!

Smooch!

Then he strutted over to us.

"The ladies like you," said Olive.

"It *is* a gift," Ben replied.

"Time to go," I said. It wasn't very polite. But that's the kind of thing you say when you're the only crab in the sea.

CHAPTER NINE

TEN MINUTES LATER, WE were back out on the sidewalk, heading down Augusta Street.

"Hey, why are we walking so fast?" asked Olive. "Where's the fire?"

That was an expression my dad always used. I could feel my mood getting worse, the bats flapping harder in my belly. Gritting my teeth, I nodded toward Ben, who was once again dressed in his goofy colonial getup. "Why do you think?"

"I think we're hurrying to get . . ." Olive

grinned. "ICE CREAM!" She pointed to the Long John Shivers truck parked at the curb.

"Did you say ice cream?" said Ben. "The last time I sampled that scrumptious delicacy was while visiting Governor Fauquier at his palace in New Jersey. Just before dinner, a summer storm erupted, producing enough hail for the servants to create a most astonishing strawberry confection." He smacked his lips at the memory. "I confess I have not tasted anything like it since."

"You should try the Jelly Roger," said Olive. "It's my favorite. Strawberry ice cream with strawberry jam and strawberry sprinkles. It's pink." Grabbing his hand, she tugged him over to the order window. "What do you want, Nolan?" she called back to me.

"I want to go home," I said. "We *need* to get home."

"I'll get your usual." She turned to the ice cream man, who was wearing an eye patch and a fake parrot on his shoulder. "Two Jelly Rogers and a vanilla cone."

At least she remembered my favorite.

The ice cream man handed the treats out the window. "That'll be four dollars."

Olive turned to me expectantly.

With a sigh, I reached into my jeans pocket.

"Allow me," said Ben. He pulled out a strange-looking bill and handed it through the window.

"Hey, old man, what are you trying to pull?" asked the ice cream man. "This isn't real money."

"It most certainly *is,* good sir," retorted Ben. "That is a ten-shilling note. It is legal tender in all the American colonies. I should know. I printed it myself."

The ice cream man stuck his head out the window so he and his fake parrot could look Ben in the eye. "You want to know what I do with homemade money, *good sir*? Watch this." He wadded Ben's bill into a ball and tossed it into the trash can.

The fake parrot rocked back and forth. It kind of looked like it was laughing.

"How dare you toss away legitimate money?" demanded Ben. He held the ice cream with one hand and put the other sternly on his hip. "Fie on you, sir!"

"Oh, yeah?" replied the ice cream man. He flipped up his eye patch and made a fist.

I pushed between them. "I got it," I said, handing up four singles.

The ice cream man took the bills. "Crazy old coot," he grumbled under his breath. Flipping his eye patch back down, he slammed the window shut.

"What an impolite fellow," muttered

Ben. He turned away and took a bite of his ice cream. "Mmmm, but he does serve a delicious confection."

"I told you so," said Olive through pink-smeared lips.

We strolled through the town park. It was the middle of the afternoon, and people lounged on the shaded benches, escaping the heat. Kids climbed on the playground

equipment. Dogs panted under the trees. A
teenager slooshed by on a skateboard.

Ben watched her, transfixed. "A decidedly
odd form of amusement," he finally com-
mented.

"I can ollie," said Olive.

"No, you can't," I said.

"If I owned a skateboard I could," she
retorted.

Oh, brother.

"Who, pray tell, is Ollie?" asked Ben.

"It's not a who, it's a what," began Olive.

I interrupted. "Just forget it." I could feel peoples' eyes boring into us. "Let's walk faster, okay?"

"On the contrary," said Ben. "Let us sit a moment." He lowered himself to a bench with a loud sigh and an even louder . . .

TOOT!

"Ewww, gross," said Olive.

"The best of all medicines are rest and farting," replied Ben. He took a last lick of his ice cream.

Olive made a face. "I'm going to go swing."

"We have to go," I reminded her. "And *soon*."

"Yeah, yeah." She raced to the playground, a trail of melty pink drops marking her path.

Ben patted the bench space next to him.

The last thing I wanted was to sit. But Ben looked tired. I guess stunt swimming, not to mention traveling almost three hundred years, will do that to a guy.

"Do you promise to stop . . . uh . . . *that*?" I asked.

"I shall strive to control the whirlwinds in my bowels," he replied.

I perched with my half-eaten cone at the far end of the bench. I hoped I was upwind.

"Tell me," said Ben. "Was that a likeness of my good friend George Washington on the money you gave that peddler?"

"He's on the dollar bill," I said, catching a vanilla drip with my tongue. "Other denominations have other faces."

"Famous faces, I presume."

I nodded. "Famous Americans. You know, people who did important stuff." I twirled the cone around in my mouth. "Abraham Lincoln is on the five-dollar bill."

Ben sniffed. "Him again."

"Don't feel bad," I said. "You're on the front of the hundred-dollar bill."

"You don't say? One hundred dollars?" His face lit and he turned to me. "I should very much like to see one of these bills."

"Wouldn't we all," I said.

From the playground, Olive shouted, "Hey, Ben! Watch this!" She hung upside down on the monkey bars.

"Be careful, young miss!" he hollered back. Then he said to me, "You know, Nolan, my daughter was once a little girl like Olive—high-spirited and full of fun. Sally, we called her. She is grown now."

"I'm an orangutan!" cried Olive. She scratched under her arms and hooted like an ape.

"I also have two . . . ahem . . . I mean, had *one* son," said Ben. For a split second he looked kind of lost. Then his confusion, or whatever it was, cleared. He went on.

"Dearest Franky, stolen from his mother and me by smallpox at age four. To this day I cannot think of my little boy without a sigh."

He gazed at Olive, who was now swooping back and forth on a swing, shouting, "I'm flying! I'm flying!"

"I missed most of Sally's childhood," he finally said. "At first I was too much occupied with my printing business and my electrical experiments to spend time with her. Then I journeyed to London on behalf of Pennsylvania's colonists to take up the matter of taxes." He paused. "I did not expect to be away from home for seventeen years. By the time I returned, we were strangers."

"Our dad is in London," I said. "He moved there two months ago. My parents are getting a divorce."

Right away, I wished I hadn't told him that. Believe me, talking about the divorce was not something I did. *Ever.* When my friends asked why they didn't see my dad around anymore, I just told them he'd gone away on a business trip. A *long* business trip. Even Tommy Tuttle hadn't ferreted out that secret yet.

Ben watched me for a long moment. "Ah, Nolan," he finally said. He laid his hand on my shoulder.

I didn't brush it off.

We sat there together, each of us lost in our own thoughts, until Olive came running back. She wiggled in between us. "Oooh, comfy cozy."

Ben smiled. "Snug as a bug in a rug."

I have to admit, it *was* pretty nice. I leaned back, letting myself relax. I even joined in when Olive started humming "Yankee Doodle."

"Oh, how jolly," said Ben. "I know that tune."

"I just bet you do," came a familiar voice. Then the branches of a nearby lilac bush started to shake. A second later, Tommy Tuttle, wearing a camouflage jumpsuit and a pair of binoculars around his neck, stepped out in front of us.

I shook my head in bewilderment. What was with this kid and bushes? And where did he buy those clothes?

Olive looked at him and pointed. "Were you peeing in there?"

"What? No!" snapped Tommy, his cheeks turning red. "I was staking you out. See?" He held up a notebook labeled *Crime-Solving Journal*. "I've had you three under surveillance all morning."

"Under what?" asked Olive.

Tommy ignored her question. "I took detailed notes on everything I saw and heard," he went on. "And believe me, chumps, what I saw and heard was beyond strange."

"Hey!" huffed Olive. "He called me a chimp!"

"Chump," I corrected her. "And who says *chump* anymore?"

"Both words sound most impolite," added Ben.

I tried to act casual. "I don't get what's so

strange," I said. "We've been to the library and the pool, had some ice cream." I shrugged. "Seems like an ordinary summer's day in Rolling Hills to me."

"There's more to it than that." From the pages of his notebook, Tommy pulled out a small square of paper. "And *this* proves it."

I recognized it right away. It was the shilling note Ben had printed; the one the ice cream man had thrown into the trash can.

Tommy waved the money triumphantly. "Now what do you say, hmmm?"

"I say you're a sneaky little snoop!" hollered Olive.

"Sneaky is in my blood," replied Tommy with a little smile. "My grandfather is a security guard."

I was stunned. He really *had* watched us all day. My mouth opened and shut, opened and . . . I blurted out the first thing that came into my head. "Yeah? Well . . . um . . . *my* grandfather is a dog groomer. That doesn't make me Skippyjon Jones."

"Huh?" said Olive. "I thought Grampy was an accountant."

"Who, pray tell, is this Skippyjon Jones?" asked Ben.

"Forget it," I muttered.

Tommy started strutting around in front of us like a lawyer in some courtroom drama. "This *is* colonial money. It's real. I know because I looked it up on Factopedia. It came from *his* pocket." Pointing at Ben, he paused to let the words sink in before adding, "So where did he get colonial money? There's only one explanation: he brought it with him from colonial times."

"Maybe he bought it at the Antique Barn over on Linden Street," I said.

"Yeah," Olive cut in. "The Antique Barn on Linden. Bet you didn't think of that."

"The Antique Barn went out of business," said Tommy. "I know because I looked in the windows." He stroked his chin. "So just how did Benjamin Franklin and his money get here? Hmmmm?" He was silent a moment. Then the corners of his mouth turned up. "There's only one way to find out the truth."

"Oh, yeah, like what, Detective Dork?" I said. "A hidden camera? A bugging device? Maybe you could just ask George Washington." It wasn't a great line, I know. But I was nervous. I didn't like the sly look on Tommy's face.

"There are better ways," he replied. "Yes, much better ways." And turning on his heel, he abruptly walked away.

"Butt head!" Olive hollered after him.

TOOOT!

We looked at Ben. His face was red with glee. "I obviously and heartily agree," he said with a giggle.

"Gross," said Olive, giggling too.

I didn't join in. Instead, I watched as Tommy hurried out of the park, past the ice cream truck, and down Augusta Street. "We should go home," I said.

"And let that meanie ruin our day? No way," said Olive. She flung her arms wide and exclaimed, "Last one to the fire station is a rotten egg!"

She took off running.

CHAPTER TEN

SINCE ROLLING HILLS IS located smack-dab in the middle of Illinois—the flattest place on earth—the town isn't exactly rolling. Or hilly. In fact, it only has one little hill (my teacher last year, Mr. Druff, calls it a hillock), and the fire station is built on top of it. Today, the station's garage doors stood wide open, displaying Rolling Hills's one and only fire truck to passersby. Brave and red, the truck's spotless chrome and brass glinted in the sunlight.

Ben stopped short in his buckled shoes.

He gasped. He pointed. He squealed like a little kid. "Oh, look yonder!"

The truck's bright reflection flickered in Ben's glasses, and his face beamed with joy and excitement. "It is fantastic. How I wish my fire company had such a conveyance."

"Yeah, it is real shiny, but we really don't have time to stop," I said. I was still worrying about Tommy.

Just then, a troop of wide-eyed little kids came down the sidewalk. Each clutching their buddy's hand, they shuffled toward us two by two, like some weird version of the animals boarding Noah's ark. Each of them had on a yellow T-shirt that read PITTER-PATTER DAY CAMP and a red construction paper name tag shaped like a fire hydrant.

The kids looked slightly lost, gazing here and there, bunching up when they stopped. One boy, whose hydrant identified him as Paulie, asked, "Where are we?"

"It's the fire station," chirped their counselor, who also wore a fire hydrant. Hers read

"Miss Missy." A wide, white-toothed smile spread across her face. "We're here to meet Fire Chief Sid and see the fire truck, remember?"

"Fire trucks are dumb," grumped Paulie.

"Yeah, dumb," said his buddy, whose hydrant read "Braydon."

"I like digger trucks," grumbled Paulie.

"Yeah, digger trucks," said Braydon.

Paulie scrunched up his face. "Stop copying me!" he howled. "Miss Missy, he's copying me."

"And I like cupcakes," said Braydon.

The other kids nodded. "Mmmm, cupcakes."

"People, we are talking about trucks here," Paulie corrected them. "Cupcakes are not trucks." His little hands turned into little fists.

"Now, now." Miss Missy playfully wagged a finger at the boys. "Come on, you two. Turn those frowns upside down."

Braydon smiled.

But Paulie stuck out his lower lip.

"Come along, gloomy Gus," said Miss Missy.

"My name's not Gus, it's Paulie." He looked down at his name tag, squinting closely at the letters. "*D . . . E . . . N . . . 3 . . . X . . . F.* See? That spells Paulie."

Miss Missy burst into song. "The happy train is coming. Get on board. *Choo-choo!*" She tugged on an imaginary whistle. "The happy train is coming. Get on board. . . ."

"*Choo-choo!*" chimed in the other preschoolers.

A boy named Kevin pulled his finger out of his nose and pointed it at Paulie. "Gus didn't *choo-choo,*" he tattled.

"It's Paulie," cried Paulie. "*D . . . E . . . N—*"

By this time the other kids were beginning to wander distractedly. We found ourselves surrounded.

"Are you the oatmeal man?" a girl labeled Gloria asked Ben.

Olive giggled. "He looks like the man on the Quaker Oats box, but he's really—"

"You dress funny," piped up Kevin, poking Ben in the belly with the same finger that had been up his nose.

"I can tell you eat cupcakes too," said Braydon.

"Mmmm, cupcakes," said the other kids.

"I like corn," said a boy whose hydrant read "Clarence." "I eat corn every night."

Miss Missy clapped her hands. "Boys and girls, look who's here. It's Fire Chief Sid!"

"Hooray, Fire Chief Sid!" chimed the kids. They swarmed around a smiling firefighter who'd come out onto the sidewalk carrying a stack of toy hats.

"Let's get a fire hat," said Olive.

"Hats?" squealed Ben. "There are hats?"

Oh, brother.

We joined the group of kids just as Fire Chief Sid tried to put a hat on Paulie's head. "Here you go, kiddo."

He pushed it away. "You got construction hats? I like construction trucks."

The Chief looked down at Paulie, not knowing what to say.

"I like dinosaurs," said a girl named Kristen.

"Me too," said Braydon.

"I like race cars," added a boy named Kwame.

"Me too," said Braydon.

"Puppies!"

"Sharks!"

"Corn!"

Miss Missy clap-clapped. "Boys and girls, where are your manners?"

Gloria looked around. "They must have ranned away."

Still, the kids quieted down.

Fire Chief Sid passed out hats. "One for you," he said. "And one for you. And one for . . ." He did a double take when he got to Ben. "Aren't you a little old for toy hats?"

Ben bristled. "I may look old, but I assure you I am young at heart."

The chief looked Ben up and down, taking in his fur hat and silk breeches. He turned to me. "Is he pulling my leg?"

"Good sir, I have most assuredly *not* touched your leg," replied Ben.

"The oat man can have my hat," said Paulie.

"Give one to the oat man," said Gloria.

Suddenly, the whole group began chanting, "Oat man! Oat man!"

"Corn!" shrieked Clarence.

Looking a little panicked, Chief Sid handed a hat to Ben. "Well . . . I guess if you're with the kids."

Right away, Ben whipped off his fur cap and put on the plastic one. "Tell me, Nolan, do I look like a fireman of the twenty-first century?"

No, I thought. But I didn't say it out loud. He acted so proud I didn't have the heart to tell him how dorky he looked.

The group drifted inside following the chief, and Ben and Olive drifted right along with them. I followed. We stopped beside the big red fire truck.

"Here are some of the tools we use to fight fires," the chief said in a teacherly voice. He pointed to a long spearlike object. "Does anyone know what that tool is called?"

"Is it a laser sword?" a girl labeled "Abby" asked hopefully.

"It is a pike pole," said Ben. He turned to me. "Some tools haven't changed in centuries."

Fire Chief Sid flashed Ben an annoyed look before continuing. "And who knows what we use this tool for? Any guesses?"

"To defeat the evil empire," said Abby.

"To pick corn," said Clarence.

"We use it to reach, hold, and pull during

fires," said Ben. He blushed modestly. "I confess I am highly trained in the art of the pole. My fire company meets and trains monthly at the Royal Standard Tavern."

The kids looked from the chief to Ben and back to the chief.

Chief Sid rubbed his forehead like he was getting a headache. He turned and pointed.

"Hoses!" cried Ben before the chief could even ask his question.

"Ax!" he shouted a few moments later.

"Maybe the oat man should be the chief," said Paulie.

"Maybe you should stop answering all the questions," I whispered to Ben.

Ben shook his head. "Knowledge should never be extinguished."

Ignoring both Paulie and Ben, the chief opened the door on the driver's side of the fire truck. "Who wants to sit inside?"

The kids' faces brightened. But before they could even raise their hands—

"Oooh, me, me!" exclaimed Ben. He pushed his way to the front of the group.

Fire Chief Sid put out his hand to stop him. "Just the children," he said sternly.

"Well . . . yes . . . um . . . of course," said Ben. He stepped back.

We watched for a few minutes as kid after kid was boosted up into the driver's seat. The chief let them honk the horn and turn on the red and blue emergency lights. Gloria even got to try out the siren, but its sudden, piercing howl was startling.

"Turn it off!" screamed Paulie, plugging his ears.

"Turn it off!" screamed Braydon.

"Stop copying me!" shrieked Paulie.

"Corn!" shrieked Clarence.

It was like some sort of four-year-old battle cry or something, because instantly the kids started screeching, bumping, crawling, shoving.

Kristen pretended to be a T. rex. *"Grrrrr!"*

Abby pulled out an imaginary laser sword. *"Schrmmmm!"*

Kevin stuck his finger up his nose. "I'm picking a winner."

Olive, Ben, and I ducked for cover behind the still-open door of the fire truck.

"Phew," exclaimed Olive. "It's crazy out there."

"Such pandemonium reminds me of my days in Congress," agreed Ben. "Indeed, that little nose picker is the spitting image of John Adams." Behind his bifocals, his eyes took on a faraway look, like he was about to launch into a story.

Miss Missy's chirping broke into his thoughts.

She raised two fingers in the air. "The quiet sign is up!"

The kids paid no attention. They kept squealing and running and growling and picking. All over the fire station garage.

Miss Missy frantically clap-clap-clap-clapped her hands. "One . . . two . . . three. Eyes on me!"

The kids bumped and banged and pinballed off one another.

"I'll take care of this," said Chief Sid. He put his hands on his hips and bellowed sternly, "Children, refrain from this horse-play . . . at once!"

They flung their plastic hats at him.

Chief Sid shouted a word I can't repeat.

But the kids did. Like a chorus of naughty parrots, they said the word over and over at the top of their voices.

"Now you've done it!" cried Miss Missy.

Then she clap-clapped her hands again. "Language! Language! Take a deep belly breath, children. Find your good words."

The kids liked the bad one better.

By this time, Chief Sid had really had it. He stormed over to a side door that led into the station's yard and flung it open. "Everybody OUT!" he thundered.

Paulie, who was still standing with his ears plugged, jumped about a foot. Then he started crying. Loud.

Miss Missy picked him up. She whirled on the chief. "What kind of person goes around screaming at children?"

Chief Sid just pointed.

"Corn!" shrieked Clarence. He tumbled out the door.

The kids swarmed out after him.

"Boys and girls, where's your buddy?" Miss Missy frantically called to them as she stumbled over the threshold. "Find your buddy!"

"Buddies are dumb," whimpered Paulie.

Then Chief Sid slammed the door behind them. Leaning against it, he rubbed his face, obviously forgetting all about us. "Headache," he muttered. "Aspirin." He staggered away.

We were alone with the fire truck.

Olive looked at Ben.

Ben looked at Olive.

"Oh, no you don't," I said.

But Olive was already scrambling up into the truck's cab.

Panting, Ben clambered up behind her. He settled himself in the driver's seat. "Just look at all these marvelous folderols!" he exclaimed.

"Don't touch anything," I cautioned.

"Oh, but I would not dream of it, my boy," said Ben. He adjusted his plastic hat so it tilted over one eye and placed his hands on either side of the steering wheel. "Vroom! Vroom!"

Ben looked so happy, I had to grin.

"Come in with us, Nolan," begged Olive. "It's so cool."

"It is most decidedly, shall we say, cool," said Ben.

"Come on, Nolan," urged Olive. "Just for a second."

What could it hurt? Glancing around to make sure no one was looking, I climbed into the cab.

"Hooray!" cried Olive.

Ben wiggled over to make room.

I pulled the heavy door shut behind me.

Ben was right. There were lots of folderols. And it *was* cool.

I gripped the big steering wheel, just managing to see over it. Outside on the sidewalk, a kid in a camouflage jumpsuit stopped in front of the station. Straddling a blue bike,

he stared at the fire truck. Then he saw us in the cab, and his eyebrows rose all the way to his bushy hairline.

"Hey, there's Tommy Tuttle," said Olive. She leaned forward to peer through the big windshield. "And *there's* our crystal radio!"

Tucked into the front basket of Tommy's

bike lay a familiar wooden box. Its gold initials, "H.H.," glittered in the sunlight.

Over the truck's wide hood, Tommy and I locked eyes. Then he leaped back onto his bike and pedaled away.

"No," I said, slamming my fist on the steering wheel. "No, no, no!"

The last slam hit the gear stick.

There was a clicking sound.

And a grinding noise.

And a *thump–thump–whump*.

Then the fire truck inched out the big double door. Slowly.

"Whoa! Whoa!" I cried, grabbing at the gear stick. I tried to yank it back into place, but it refused to budge.

"Zoons, but this is most exciting!" exclaimed Ben. "My first trip in a modern conveyance. Oh, but the speed is dizzying."

"Whee!" whooped Olive.

At the top of the driveway, at the top of the hill, the truck seemed to pause. Then it . . .

Dipped . . .

Lurched . . .

Picked up speed as it rolled down the street.

Ahead of us we could see Tommy, pumping furiously.

"Oh, my, my," said Ben.

"Whoopee!" cried Olive.

"Get out of the way!" I hollered. I laid on the horn.

"*WAAAAAAAAAAH!*" it bellowed.

Tommy looked over his shoulder and his

mouth dropped open. Did he think we were chasing him? Facing forward again, he lowered his head into the wind and began pumping away like an Olympic bicyclist.

Ahead of us loomed a busy four-way stop.

Tommy took a sharp right.

It was all I could do to grip the steering wheel and keep the truck on the road.

"Might I suggest you slow down?" asked Ben.

"Brakes! Brakes!" cried Olive.

But my foot didn't reach the pedal.

"Watch out!" Ben and Olive shrieked in unison. They grabbed each other as the truck barreled through the intersection.

Brakes squealed.

Horns blared.

The sudden wail of a police car grew louder and louder.

Hopping a curb, the truck bumped up onto the sidewalk and across a grassy stretch of the city park straight toward—

"Watch out!" yelled a lady walking a poodle.

I closed my eyes.

But the crash never came. Instead, the big truck lurched, bounced, and slowed. With a final jerk, it came to a stop just inches from the town statue of Abraham Lincoln with its chiseled quote: WITH MALICE TOWARD NONE; WITH CHARITY FOR ALL.

I clung to the steering wheel, dazed, my heart pounding. "Is everybody okay?" I croaked.

Ben mopped his brow with his handkerchief. "Yes." He managed a weak nod.

"Let's do it again!" squealed Olive.

"There will be no more stunts," said a stern voice.

Slowly, I turned to look out the driver's window.

There stood Officer Nittles, her hands on her hips.

I gulped and stared at her shiny badge. Her utility belt. The big gun holstered at her hip. I rolled down the window. "Um . . . hi?" I said.

Officer Nittles comes to my school every year to hand out sticker badges and coloring sheets and teach the Friendly Police Program.

She was not looking too friendly now.

She opened the cab door. "Step out of the vehicle, gentlemen," she said to Ben and me.

"Me too?" asked Olive.

"You too," said Officer Nittles.

CHAPTER ELEVEN

IT DIDN'T TAKE LONG for a crowd to gather. Neighbors. Passersby. Even the Long John Shivers ice cream guy. Within minutes, his truck—blaring "Yo ho ho!" from the speaker atop its roof—pulled over to the curb. I guess gapers buy ice cream. Fire Chief Sid was there, too, looking like he was about to have a complete meltdown. So were some of the other firefighters from the station.

The three of us stood stiffly in one spot as the chief, his men, and Officer Nittles walked around and around the truck, inspecting it for damage. From behind us came the static and chatter of the police car's radio.

The radio! It felt like a hundred years ago that the mysterious package had arrived . . . followed by Ben . . . followed by that big snoop Tommy . . . followed by *this*.

"H.H.," I muttered under my breath. Who was he? Why had he sent me that radio? His gift, if that's what it was supposed to be, had brought nothing but trouble. Big trouble.

Finally, Officer Nittles returned to us. She pulled out her notebook. "Want to tell me what happened?"

"They crashed my truck!" barked Chief Sid.

"I'd like to hear what they have to say," said Officer Nittles.

My stomach churned. I was dizzy. All day long—no, all summer long, since Dad left—I'd been trying to hold things together. But it was all unraveling now. A lump grew in my throat.

"There's nothing to say," I said at last.

Officer Nittles looked at Ben and Olive. "What about you two?"

"We didn't mean to do it," explained Olive.

"I merely wanted to sit in that marvelous conveyance for a moment," added Ben.

"We accidentally bumped a stick and it just started moving," Olive went on.

"I am, I confess, woefully unfamiliar with the workings of your modern vehicles," said Ben.

Olive nodded. "He's really old." She

paused a second, then added, "And I'm only seven."

Officer Nittles raised her eyebrows. "Anything else?"

"Umm . . . I like your shoes?" said Olive.

I swear Officer Nittles almost smiled. But it didn't change anything. She gestured for Chief Sid to join her by her squad car. I couldn't hear what they were saying, but I figured it wasn't good. Their expressions were serious, and their heads were bent close together. Chief Sid was doing most of the talking. Officer Nittles took lots of notes.

I broke into a cold sweat. How many years did a person get for stealing a fire truck, anyway?

I'd grow thin on bread and water.

I'd have to wear an orange jumpsuit, even though orange is *not* a good color for me. It makes me look like a squash.

Mom's next book would be titled *The Bumble Bunnies Break Their Mother's Heart.*

I was trembling by the time Officer Nittles returned to us. "Time to go for a little ride, you three," she said.

I could feel my eyes getting wet. Beside me, Olive started sniffling. Ben patted her arm.

"Um . . . okay . . . but could you do us a favor? Please?" I wiped my nose on the sleeve of my T-shirt. "Could you wait until we're in the car to handcuff us? It would be humiliating to be handcuffed in front of all these people."

Officer Nittles's face grew puzzled. "Handcuffs are for people who are under arrest."

I winced. "I know."

"You aren't being arrested," she said. "Not that what you did wasn't serious. But no one was hurt, and no damage was done. Chief Sid has agreed not to press charges."

I couldn't believe it. I looked over at Chief Sid.

He nodded.

"You're not taking us to jail?" exclaimed Olive.

"I'm taking you home," said Officer Nittles. "I want to talk with your parents about your stupid stunt."

"Parent," I said. "Just our mom."

And she was going to be so disappointed in me.

Officer Nittles opened the back door of the squad car. She put her hand on my shoulder. "Time to go."

The three of us slid into the backseat and slumped down.

Just then, Miss Missy and the little day

camp kids rounded the corner. I guess it had taken her that long to get them back into two-by-two order.

"Hey," cried Kevin. He took his finger out of his nose and pointed. "The oat man is going to jail."

"That's dumb," said Paulie, frowning at Officer Nittles. Then he raised a little fist in the air and, smiling at Ben, shouted, "Free the oat man!"

The others raised their little fists, too.

As we pulled away, our ears filled with the chant, "Free the oat man! Free the oat man! Free the oat man!"

"Corn!" cried Clarence.

CHAPTER TWELVE

IN CASE YOU'RE WONDERING, the backseat of a police car stinks. It's a disgusting blend of pine air freshener and sweat from hundreds of bad guys. I felt a wave of nausea that had nothing to do with the car's smell. Fear makes me queasy. And just thinking about Mom's response when she saw the police at the door made me want to puke. I put my hand over my mouth. My mother is not a reasonable person about stuff like this. Like someday, we will never, ever look back on this and laugh.

Beside me, Olive said weakly, "It's all over. Seven years of being the perfect child down the toilet." She pretended to flush. *"Foosh!"*

For once, Ben was quiet. His head was bowed, his toy fire hat lying in his lap. Somewhere, he'd lost his fur cap. The fire station, maybe? Now that he was hatless, I could see the big pink bald spot on top of his head.

He must have felt me staring, because he turned and said, "I am sorry about this, Nolan—truly." He touched my sleeve. "My enthusiasms do run away with me at times."

I couldn't answer because my hand still covered my mouth. Instead, I looked out the window. The squad car turned onto my street.

Officer Nittles pulled up in front of our house, then turned to look at us through the wire mesh that separated the front and back seats. "Is this it?"

I nodded gloomily.

She got out of the car and opened the backseat door.

"We're dead," I groaned.

"Before I ever got to Disney World," muttered Olive.

I sat there.

"The sooner we do this, the sooner it's done," said Officer Nittles.

She was right. Straightening my shoulders, I jumped out of the car and strode toward the house. Boldly at first. Then slower and slower, until I came to a complete stop. I turned and looked back.

Ben took Olive's hand.

Olive took a deep breath.

Then, side by side, we began the long, nervous walk to the front door.

Officer Nittles rang the bell.

We waited.

"Are you sure your mother is home?" Officer Nittles asked.

I nodded glumly. "She's home. She's just working."

"She's blank," added Olive.

"What . . . ?" began Officer Nittles. Then she shook her head. "Forget it." She rang the doorbell again.

After what seemed like a year, Mom answered the door.

She looked from Olive to me to Officer Nittles to Ben. And the expression on her face went from surprise to worry to outright confusion. Then she held open the door, and we all stepped into the entry hall.

"What's this all about?" Mom asked. "Is everyone all right?"

"Your children and their . . . um . . . friend here were picked up this afternoon," said Officer Nittles.

"Picked up?" Mom repeated.

"They were involved in a traffic incident," said Officer Nittles. Flipping open her notebook, she started telling our mother about our "stupid stunt."

The look on Mom's face turned downright scary. Her eyes became slits, and her cheeks were sucked almost completely into her head. I'd never seen her so furious.

Jail was starting to look really good.

I tried blurting out the truth. "Mom, I can explain. It all started this morning when Ben Franklin—"

"Popped up!" Olive broke in.

"Popped up," said Mom. "Ben Franklin."

Officer Nittles nodded. "Mr. . . . ahem . . .

'Franklin's' fascination with fire trucks is what precipitated the incident," she stated.

"For which I am abjectly sorry," said Ben. He leaned toward my mother. "I am, you know, the founder of the first fire company in the American colonies."

Mom blinked.

"He made the first library, too," Olive piped up.

"And discovered electricity," I added.

Officer Nittles consulted her notebook. "Mr. Franklin gave a performance at the public library earlier today," she stated.

Mom looked into each of our faces, one by one. The muscles in her face started to relax. "I *see*," she finally said. Then she did the weirdest thing. She *smiled*. And it wasn't one of those tight-lipped, I'm-so-going-to-kill-my-kid-when-this-person-is-gone smiles, either. It was a genuine, friendly smile.

And honestly? It made me queasier than

if she *had* gone ballistic. I mean, I'd expected her to start yelling and lecturing me about acting responsibly. I'd braced myself for being grounded forever, or at least until I was thirty and too old to enjoy life. But she didn't even stare at me like she was trying to figure out where she had gone wrong with my up-bringing. She just kept smiling through the rest of the policewoman's account. A couple times she even giggled.

It was weird.

At last, Officer Nittles snapped her notebook shut. "Obviously, we won't be pressing charges on this occasion. We'd rather not take it any further if it can be dealt with at home."

"Oh, yes, of course," said Mom with a chuckle. She lowered her voice and added, "You make a very convincing policewoman."

"Pardon?" said Officer Nittles.

Mom winked. "You had me there for a minute. But I get it now. I know what's going on."

"I'm glad you grasp the situation," said Officer Nittles.

"Oh, yes," said Mom, "I certainly do."

"Then I expect you'll keep a close eye on these three."

"Absolutely," said Mom.

The policewoman left.

And Mom whirled. "You never quit, do you, Nolan? Oh, you sweet, sweet boy," she cried. Opening her arms wide, she wrapped all of us—even Ben—into a big family hug. "You are the best children in the world. What did I do to deserve you? What? What? What?" She punctuated the *what*s with kisses—one for each of us.

Ben liked this a lot, I could tell, because when she finally let go, his eyes were twinkling and his lips were puckered up like he was expecting another smooch.

"*Énchanté, madame,*" he said, his eyebrows waggling. "Allow me to introduce myself properly. I am Benjamin Franklin of Philadelphia."

"Of course you are." Mom giggled. "And I'm Betsy Ross."

"Surely you jest, madam," replied Ben seriously. "I know Betsy Ross. And you are most certainly not she." He turned to Olive and me. "Mistress Ross is a stout woman, and her hair—"

Mom giggled again.

The three of us looked at one another. What was happening?

"Nolan, you're too much," Mom gushed. "First that bunny costume and now . . . *this*." Waving toward Ben, she giggled a third time. "What an inspired idea—*The Bumble Bunnies Meet Benjamin Franklin*. Why didn't I think of it myself? All this time I've only thought about the bunnies in the modern world. But why not set them in history?" She snapped her fingers. "Wait . . . Wait . . . I have it! A new series! In each book they'll meet a famous American—Amelia Earhart, Dolley Madison, Abraham Lincoln."

"That fellow again," said Ben with a sniff.

"It's good, huh?" squealed Mom.

"Um . . . uh . . . good," I said. I was feeling very confused.

She looked longingly toward her studio, then back at us. "First I'll make you some supper, and then it's back to work. Thanks to you, it seems I've suddenly got a book to write."

"We can handle supper," I said.

"But I should . . . ," she began.

"Madam," said Ben. "One today is worth two tomorrows."

Olive nodded. "What he said."

"We got this one," I added.

Ben made a sick face. "Do promise me, Nolan, that you shall not serve those Sticks 'n' Stones again."

"Sprouts 'n' Stuff," I corrected him. "And I promise."

Mom hurried up the stairs. But at her

186

studio doorway she stopped. "Will you be staying long?" she asked Ben.

"I hope to be departing for 1784 shortly," he replied.

Mom giggled again, and disappeared into her studio.

"By the collision of luck and opportunity, sparks are struck and light is obtained," said Ben. He smiled. "You have made your mother very happy, Nolan."

It was like some kind of miracle or something.

CHAPTER THIRTEEN

"SO NOW WHAT?" ASKED Olive. She was staring at the spot on the kitchen table where the crystal radio used to be.

I flopped into a chair. "We have to get it back. That's what."

But how? No way was Tommy going to just hand it over. "We need a plan," I said.

We stared at each other.

"I know!" Olive shouted about a minute later. "We can be ninjas and sneak up on him and—" She karate-chopped the air. "Hiya!"

"Yeah, that'll work," I said.

We stared at each other some more.

"Disguises!" Olive shouted. "We'll disguise ourselves and steal back the radio. That's a good plan, huh? We can wear our costumes from last Halloween."

"Oh sure," I said with a snort. "A mummy, a mermaid princess, and a Founding Father strolling down the sidewalk. Nobody's going to notice that."

She stuck out her tongue at me.

We went back to staring.

But a minute later—

"Hypnotize him! Attack him with water pistols! Catch him in a giant butterfly net!

Drop an iron cage over him! Jump on him with jet-propelled pogo sticks!"

Oh, brother.

Ben smiled. "Those are all most ingenious plans, Olive," he said. "But there are times when brains are preferable to brawn."

"Huh?" said Olive.

"I think Ben means he has a plan," I said.

Ben's eyes twinkled. "Indeed I do, young Nolan."

"What are we going to do?" asked Olive, hopping up and down.

"He who can have patience can have what he will," said Ben. "In the meantime, this is what I need from you and Nolan."

And he sent us scurrying all over the house for bits and parts and pieces. After a few trips we had collected a big pile of stuff on the kitchen floor. There were scraps of

wire, a roll of tinfoil, and a silk scarf. There were two bent curtain rods, a broken waffle iron, a set of metal salt-and-pepper shakers shaped like the Empire State Building, two

knitting needles, five brass thimbles, an assortment of glass jars, and a hand-crank ice cream maker. There was also a saw and a hammer, nuts and bolts, a screwdriver, a bent silver fork, and a bamboo fishing pole.

Ben snapped the fishing pole in half and wrapped one end with tinfoil. "A makeshift cane . . . of sorts," he said with a grin. Then he set to work connecting and fastening the other items.

"Screwdriver, if you please, Nolan," he said, holding out his hand like a surgeon in an operating room. "Olive, will you be so kind as to place your finger here so I may tie this knot?"

Together we yanked and jimmied and pulled away the waffle iron's metal plates and fit them inside the ice cream maker. As we worked, an unexpected feeling—part happy, part sad—came over me. I remembered the time Dad and I had put together my first bicycle.

After a few more minutes, Ben waved at his invention. "I give you the electrostatic machine."

"What's it do?" asked Olive.

"Allow me to demonstrate." Ben cranked the ice cream maker's handle. A low humming came from the whirling waffle iron plates inside. The two glass jars we'd

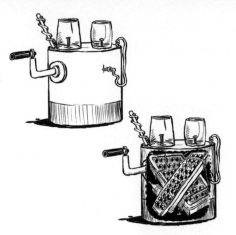

mounted on top began to vibrate. Then—

Sizzle!

Snap!

Blue sparks appeared. They bounced and crackled inside the jar.

"Pretty!" gushed Olive.

"It's like little lightning," I said.

"It is lightning, although man-made. Indeed, lad, it really is nothing more than a parlor trick. Would you like to try?" He handed me one of the knitting needles.

"How?"

"Merely hold it near," he said, gesturing.

I held the needle out slowly. When it got within an inch of the machine, a tiny blue-white bolt of electricity leaped from the glass jars to the tip of my needle. Instantly, I felt a tingling in my hand. I jumped back, dropping the needle.

"Did it hurt?" asked Olive.

I shook my head. "Not really. It was just a surprise."

"I call it a 'kiss,'" said Ben. "An 'electric kiss.'"

"I want to try," said Olive. She grabbed a knitting needle. A second later, little lightning bolts were flashing toward her.

"Ooooh, tingly," she said.

She held the needle in place.

"Kiss me again!"

Snap! Sizzle! Zap!

"Enough now, Olive," said Ben. "We still have work to do." He turned to me. "Might you have a gripsack or satchel about?"

"A what?" I asked.

"Oooh, wait, I know," cried Olive. She raced up to her bedroom and returned with her Princess Aquamarina Shimmer and Sparkle Backpack. The mermaid's tail twinkled and flashed with every step she took. She held it up so Ben could see. "You mean something like this?"

"Exactly," he said. "May I?"

Olive handed it to him.

"What's that for?" I asked.

Ben gestured for us to come close. He whispered his plan.

"That idea is almost as good as a giant butterfly net!" Olive exclaimed when he was done.

I wasn't so sure. "This won't be like that

turkey experiment you told us about earlier, will it? You know, when you electrocuted yourself?"

"Fear not, dear boy," Ben reassured me. "I am highly experienced in the delivery of electrical kisses. I have often used a similar strategy to scatter the gawkers gathered in front of my house." He paused a moment before adding, "I electrified my wrought-iron fence."

"*BZZZZZZT!*" shrieked Olive. She stiffened and shook as if a shock of electricity were running through her body.

"Hardly as severe as that," replied Ben, making some adjustments to the backpack. "No, sweet Olive, my kisses are always harmless. People often squeal or jump, but they are never hurt."

"Never?" cried Olive. "But I want to *zap* Tommy. Zing him a good one! Zonk him and . . ." She smacked her fist into her palm. "Zowie!" She paused to catch her breath. "Let's shock him unconscious and grab the radio."

I rolled my eyes. So much for "sweet Olive."

She stomped her foot. "So why'd we build all this stuff if we're not going to sizzle the snoop?"

"The element of surprise," replied Ben.

"I don't get it," said Olive.

Ben explained. "Master Tuttle will not be expecting a kiss. It will surprise him. Startle him. And in that moment we shall gain the upper hand."

"And with our upper hands we grab the radio, right?" added Olive.

"Correct," said Ben.

CHAPTER FOURTEEN

IT WAS LATE AFTERNOON by the time we pulled Olive's wagon down Laurel Street. In the back, the electrostatic machine bumped and rattled. Beside it, the backpack twinkled and flashed. Ignoring the stares

from passersby, we turned onto Euclid Lane. Tommy's house sat on the corner. From our spot on the sidewalk we could see into his backyard.

"So cute!" squealed Olive, pointing to a wooden playhouse. It had a shingled roof, shutters at each of its four miniature windows, and a little deck porch. A blue bicycle leaned against the railing.

"He's in there," I said.

Olive karate-chopped the air. "Then let's get him. Hiya!"

I shook my head. "You two stay here. It's my turn to do a little surveillance."

Keeping low, I scurried across the yard to the playhouse and crouched beneath one of its little windows. Maybe I kept on breathing. I must have. But that's about all I dared to do at first. Then through the thin pane of glass I heard someone humming. Slowly, carefully, I raised myself up and peeked over the sill.

The inside of Tommy's playhouse looked like something out of a police show. There was a poster of the FBI's Most Wanted tacked to one wall, along with a framed picture of Sherlock Holmes. There was a microscope, and the periscope, and a pair of high-powered binoculars. There was a fingerprint kit, along with a roll of crime-scene tape, plastic evidence bags, specimen swabs, and a shelf full of books with titles like *DIY Private Eye* and *Spying for Dummies*.

Tommy stood in the middle of the room. He'd swapped out his camo jumpsuit for a lab coat. Obviously, he hadn't been able to get one in his size—that is, short and skinny. The coat hung down all the way to the floor. More than once he tripped over its hem as he moved around a low table, a magnifying glass pressed to his eye, to examine my crystal radio. Every few seconds, he jotted a note in his crime-solving journal.

"Do you see anything?"

Startled, I dropped back beneath the window and whirled around.

There was Olive. Behind her was Ben, pulling the wagon.

"Didn't I tell you to stay back?" I hissed at her.

"But I was curious," she said.

"As was I," added Ben.

I gestured for them to get down.

Ben crouched, his knees creaking like an unoiled door.

"Shhhh," I whispered, before adding, "The radio . . . it's in there."

"Did he make it work?" asked Olive. "Is George Washington or Abraham Lincoln or somebody like that in there with him?"

"That Lincoln fellow," sniffed Ben. "Zoons, but I'd like to have a few words with him."

"Tommy's alone," I said.

"Lucky for Mr. Lincoln," grumbled Ben.

Just in case, I crept to the corner of the playhouse and cautiously peered around. "It's all clear," I whispered back to Olive and Ben. "I'm going in."

"Me too," said Olive.

"And I," said Ben. Using the makeshift bamboo cane, he creakily stood. "Let us

retrieve the contraption immediately. Lost time is never found again, you know."

My nerves felt like Mexican jumping beans as I dragged the wagon onto the deck. Ben and Olive followed.

"Let's bash in the door," she said. She did a karate kick. "Hiya!"

Instead, I grabbed the doorknob and gave it a turn. The door swung open. The three of us burst into the playhouse.

Tommy whirled. His eyes widened for an instant, then turned squinty. "You!" he exclaimed. "I thought you three would be in jail by now."

Olive put her hands on her hips. "Well, nyah, nyah, we're not, so there."

"But *you* should be," I added. "You stole our radio."

"Stole?" said Tommy. "I didn't steal anything. I collected evidence—evidence proving that *he* is the real Benjamin Franklin."

"Give it back!" demanded Olive. She karate-chopped at him. "Give it back, or else."

Tommy snorted. "Or else what?"

"I'll kiss you," she replied.

"I'm soooo scared," drawled Tommy.

"Young man," said Ben, "we are giving

you the opportunity to right your wrong with no repercussions."

"Get lost, Franklin," said Tommy.

Ben shook his head sadly. "It appears you leave us no other course of action." He turned to my sister. "Olive, if you please."

With a nod, Olive pulled the wagon through the doorway. Then she began cranking the handle of the electrostatic machine. It whirred and hummed. Pinpricks of electricity lit up the glass jars. Then a spark suddenly danced across Ben's cane. Its metal tip vibrated.

"That will be sufficient, Olive," said Ben.

She quit cranking.

And Tommy chuckled. "What are you doing? Making ice cream?"

"No, dummy, I'm making you that kiss I promised," said Olive.

I tried again. "Come on, Tommy. Please. Just hand over the radio."

Tommy snorted. "No way, Stanberry. I'm

keeping it. That thing is going to make me the most famous kid detective in the country. I'll get my own reality show. That is, just as soon as I figure out how it works."

Ben sighed. "I had hoped you'd see reason, young man. But I can tell you mean to keep the contraption. So . . ." He set the Princess Aquamarina backpack on the floor. It shimmered and flashed as he pushed it forward with the tip of his cane.

"What's that?" Tommy stared at the backpack suspiciously. I could almost see the gears in his head turning. "Another time-travel machine?"

"Don't touch it, Tommy," I said, putting myself between him and the backpack. "Believe me, it's . . . uh . . . shocking."

"Nolan, you're ruining everything!" yelped Olive.

Ben looked me in the eye. "Don't you want to right this wrong, my boy?"

"Not this way," I said. "Sure, I know it's just a little kiss, but . . . well . . . two wrongs don't make a right."

Olive looked up at Ben. "Is that one of your sayings?"

"No, dear Olive, but it should have been." He nodded slowly. "Yes indeed, it most certainly should have been." He bent for the backpack.

"Oh, no you don't!" cried Tommy. He pushed me aside, reached out and . . .

ZAAAP!

A blue spark of electricity burst from the backpack. Crackling, it lit up the mermaid's tail like a neon sign and filled the air with the bitter smell of melting plastic before leaping up to touch Tommy's outstretched fingers.

"Yeoooow!"

Geez, was he ever surprised. As he jumped back, Tommy's feet tangled in his too-long lab coat. He stumbled. Flailed. Grabbed at the air. And landed with a crashing *THUD* on the playhouse floor. Books, specimen swabs, rubber gloves, fingerprint brushes, and evidence bags rained down around him. The Most Wanted poster fluttered down and landed on his chest. A roll of crime-scene tape bonked him on the head.

"Upper hand!" cheered Olive. Grabbing the tape, she raced around and around the still-surprised Tommy. In seconds, his arms were pinned to his sides with yellow plastic.

"I told you not to touch it," I said.

Tommy squirmed and struggled. "Let me loose," he demanded.

"Not until we've got what you stole from us," I said. Moving to the table, I picked up the radio, carried it out to the wagon, and set it beside the electrostatic machine. Then I came back inside and bent over him. I nudged him with the toe of my sneaker. "Are you okay?"

Tommy didn't say a word. He just growled at me through clenched teeth.

"Yep, he's okay," piped up Olive.

By now, Tommy's face was so red he looked like a chili pepper. For a second, I thought he might actually explode. "You . . . you *shocked* me!" he bellowed.

"What, that teensy, weensy spark?" said Olive. "That was just a little kiss. Show him how you did it, Ben."

Ben nodded and pointed toward the backpack. It no longer flashed and glittered. Now a thin trail of black smoke rose from Princess Aquamarina's once-shimmering tail. "There is a knitting needle hidden in that satchel, which young Olive charged by cranking the electrostatic machine. A wire— you see?—runs down my stick. It delivered the spark from the machine to the satchel. Your desperation for fame and recognition did the rest."

Olive stepped over Tommy and picked up her ruined backpack. "No more shimmer and shine," she said. "But it was worth it."

"I'll get you for this!" hollered Tommy. He twisted and wiggled some more, and suddenly his left index finger poked through the tape.

"Time to go," I said, herding both Ben and Olive toward the door. I knew it would only be a matter of minutes before Tommy worked himself free. And I wanted to be far away when he did.

"This isn't over, Stanberry!" Tommy shouted after me.

I had a feeling he was right.

CHAPTER FIFTEEN

IT DIDN'T TAKE LONG for us to get back home. Once again, I put the crystal radio on the kitchen table, where it sat, dark and silent.

I looked it over. "I don't think anything's

broken," I finally said. I wiped a smudge of what I thought was probably fingerprint powder off the headphones.

"Tommy sure was mad," said Olive.

Ben nodded. "I'm afraid you have made an enemy, Nolan."

I nodded.

"An archenemy," said Olive.

I nodded again.

"A forever and ever archenemy," said Olive.

"All right, already," I grumbled. "I got it."

Olive shrugged. "I'm just saying."

Ben cleared his throat "And now, my young friends, *I* must be saying good-bye."

"But I don't want you to go," Olive said. She slipped her hand into Ben's.

I admit, I felt a little sad too. Even though the day had been stressful and frustrating and downright weird, I'd sort of gotten used to having Ben around.

"I want you to stay forever and ever," said Olive.

"Tut," said Ben. "Don't you know fish and visitors stink after three days?"

She shook her head, tears welling up in her eyes. "That's dead fish. And you're here, right now, and I don't want you to go."

Ben dropped to one creaking knee and looked in her face. "You are a most singular little girl, dear Olive, and if circumstances were different, I would heartily stay with you. But I have my own home, and my own family. Did I tell you my grandchildren live with me?"

She shook her head, sniffling loudly.

"Seven little prattlers who cling about their grandpapa's knees, begging for kisses and stories." He winked. "And I have a most special tale to tell them tonight."

"About me and Nolan?"

"You have become cherished parts of my life."

She thought a moment, her lower lip poked out. Then she took a deep breath. "Okay."

214

He smiled. "I am not in so much of a hurry that I would pass up a hug. That is, if you were inclined to give one."

Olive laughed and wrapped her arms around his neck.

The two squeezed each other tight.

Then Ben slowly straightened. "Master Nolan, I place myself in your most capable hands. Where would you have us begin?"

I stood there a second. All day all I'd wanted was to fix things, make things right by sending Ben home. But now? It sounds crazy, but I didn't want him to go, either.

"Nolan?" said Ben.

I shook my head. "Oh . . . er . . . right." I looked at the radio. "I think we should do exactly what we did this morning," I finally said. "Repeat every step."

"Replicate the experiment," said Ben. "Exceedingly wise."

I couldn't help but blush. I mean, it's not every day that Ben Franklin calls you wise.

"What if I don't remember every step?" asked Olive.

"Try," I said. "Put on your thinking cap."

She did. Flopping into a kitchen chair, she pretended to tie on a hat.

I rolled my eyes. "Oh, brother."

"What would you have *me* do?" asked Ben.

"I think you should go stand over there in the doorway since that's where you first materialized or . . . beamed up or . . . whatever."

Clutching his toy fire hat to his chest, he took his place.

"Are you taking *that*?" I asked as I cleared trash and dishes off the table.

"I certainly am," said Ben. He grinned. "I seem to have misplaced my fur cap. And oh, but the fellows in the fire company are going to be most astonished."

I snorted. "They must be pretty easily impressed."

That's when Olive pulled off her thinking cap. "I remember," she announced. She reached for the radio. "First I touched this little lever right here. . . ."

"Wait a second," I said. I looked over at Ben. "You ready?"

Ben nodded. "Let the experiment be made!" he called out to us.

I waved. "Safe travels, Ben."

"Say hi to your grandkids for me," said Olive. She started blowing kisses. *"Mwah! Mwah! Mwah! Mwah! M—"*

"Can we do this already?" I interrupted. I was trying to stay focused, trying to remember the exact steps, trying not to sound like I was going to cry.

She wrinkled her nose at me and finished her smooch. *"Mwah!"* Then, as she'd done that morning, she moved the tiny brass arm. . . . I slipped on the headphones. She turned the dial.

One click.

"Adieu, dear children!" hollered Ben.

Two clicks.

"I shall never forget you."

Three clicks.

We waited for the stone to start glowing.

We waited for the headphones to fill with static.

We waited for the room to dissolve and bubbles to pop. Instead . . .

"I am still here," said Ben.

The crystal radio sat stubbornly silent.

We tried again.

And again.

Nothing happened.

"I don't get it," whined Olive "We did it exactly the same."

I peered down at the radio. All the parts were there. But suddenly—I can't explain why—I got the strangest feeling that we were missing a step. We'd forgotten to do something.

Ben sagged into a chair. For the first time all day, his eyes didn't twinkle, and his chin drooped to his chest. He let out a big sigh. "Ah, Nolan, I had never considered that in this age of wonders, I might not be able to return home."

"You can stay with us. Right, Nolan?"

Olive grabbed Ben's hand and looked at me hopefully.

I didn't know what to say. So I just stood there, not saying anything.

"He can sleep in the guest room and wear Daddy's left-behind clothes."

I doubted it. Dad's left-behind pants would have to be hemmed at least a foot, and the waistbands let *way* out.

"He could help Mom with her books. Ben knows *all* those colonial people."

I glanced up the stairs toward the studio where Mom was still working. Having Ben around *would* help her.

"And we could do experiments, and build stuff and . . . *mermaid swim!*" She flung her arms wide with excitement.

I have to admit, she made it sound pretty nice. Then I looked into Ben's sad eyes, and I knew it could never work. He had his own home and his own family. He would miss them the same way I miss Dad. He would feel like he was carrying a deep, empty hole inside.

Ben dabbed at his eyes with one lace cuff.

And Olive wrapped her skinny arms around his neck. "Don't worry, Ben. It'll be okay."

"Sure it will," I added. "All we have to do is figure out the radio." I remembered something he'd said earlier. "The scientific mind is ever questioning."

He looked up. "You are quite right, Nolan. We must undertake a thorough scientific examination of that contraption . . ."

I nodded. "That's the spirit, Ben!"

". . . tomorrow." He seemed to sag even further. "Faugh, but I am feeling dropsical."

I wasn't sure what that meant, but it didn't sound good.

Olive jumped in. "I'm hungry. Aren't you hungry, Ben? I think we should eat. I bet that would make you feel less Popsicle . . .

er ... bicycle ... um ... make you feel better."

"Good thinking, Olive!" I cried, acting like it was the greatest idea since the lightning rod.

Remembering how much he'd enjoyed those earlier pizza puffs, I microwaved up another box. Olive even brought him a tankard of ale.

"*Ginger* ale," she explained. Still, she'd poured it into a big mug so it sort of looked like the real thing.

Not that it mattered much. Ben just picked at his food. When he finished

pushing pepperoni around his plate, he went into the family room and lowered himself into my dad's old easy chair. His hands, resting on his knees, remained stone-still. Not a single finger twitched. He closed his eyes.

At the kitchen table, Olive traced the radio's gold block initials over and over. "H.H.!" she suddenly cried. "I bet he knows how the radio works."

"Yeah? And how are we going to find him?'"

"Call him? Maybe he has a phone number."

I rolled my eyes. "Oh, brother. That might be the stupidest—" I stopped. I thought a second. "Wait a minute! You might be on to something. Maybe—"

"What?"

"Maybe we can find H.H. online."

"You think H.H. has a website or a Facebook page or something?"

I shrugged. "Weirder things have happened today."

Olive touched Ben's arm. "You want to come with me? I'll let you click the mouse."

I thought for sure the phrase "click the mouse" would get him going. But he didn't even open his eyes. "No thank you, dear."

Olive's lower lip trembled. She was obviously as worried about him as I was.

She and I went into the computer room. Before the divorce, it had been Dad's study. But now all his books and papers and research materials were gone. Just empty shelves, a table and chairs, and a desktop computer remained. I booted it up and typed the initials *H.H.* into the search engine.

"Ugh," groaned Olive.

If H.H. was online, it wouldn't be easy to locate him. We found hula hoops and headless horsemen, Haircut Haven, the Hilltop Hotel, haunted houses, health hazards, H & H Plumbing Supplies. There must have been like a gazillion H.H.s.

"Horatio Hornblower," I read.

"That's a silly name," said Olive.

I tapped some keys.

"Herbert Hoover."

"Who?" said Olive.

"He was a president," I replied.

She shrugged. "Who knew?"

I scrolled through a few more screens, but I was losing hope.

"Stop!" cried Olive.

"Did you find something?"

"Hector the Hedgehog's fan club site. I love his cartoons. Can we bookmark that?"

It was useless. There were way too many possibilities.

Just then the computer let out an electronic chime.

Only one person could be video calling at this time of day.

I pushed back from the computer and

made for the door as Olive eagerly clicked some keys on the computer.

"Hi, Daddy!" she chirped.

I was almost to the door when she turned. "Nolan, come talk to Dad."

I looked back. Behind her on the computer screen I could see him smiling. "Hello? Nolan? Is that you, buddy?"

I shut the door in his video face.

Ben was leaning forward in the easy chair, his ear tuned toward the study. "You do not wish to speak with your father?" he said when he saw me.

I shook my head. "I haven't talked to him in a while," I confessed. "Not since he left."

Ben took a deep breath. He seemed to be deciding whether or not to tell me something. At last, he said, "I have another son. Did you know that, Nolan?"

"Besides Franky?"

Ben pulled a cotton cloth from his sleeve and polished his glasses. "William." He said the name softly. "Strange how the word feels on my lips. I have long refused even to utter it."

"You don't say his name?"

"I no longer speak to him either," said Ben. He shook his head. "I no longer see him."

"Ever?"

"Never." Ben's eyes took on a faraway look. "Oh, my dear, brilliant William . . ."

And he told this story.

Once upon a time, there was a beautiful little boy.

Do you see him there? His name was William Franklin, and he was the apple of my eye.

I was an indulgent father. As he grew, William wanted for nothing.

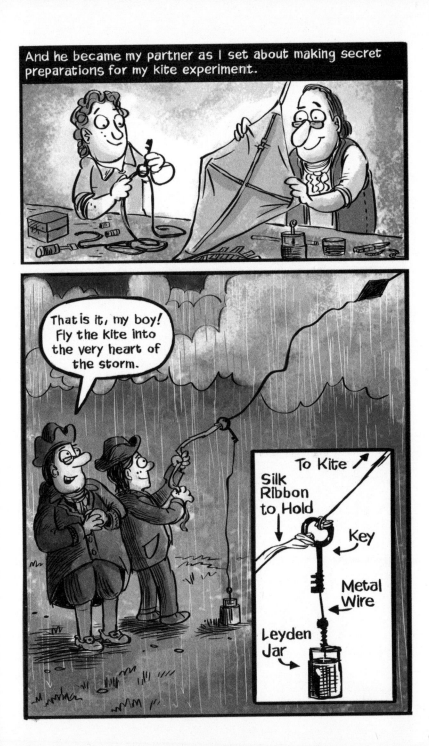

ZZZRRTt!

It is true, Father. Electricity and lightning *are* one and the same!

The success was made sweet because William was there to share it.

But then revolution came. And all colonists had to choose. Would they fight for America's freedom?

Or stay loyal to England and its king?

I chose America.

William chose the king.

Olive came out of the computer room then and curled up in a corner of the couch. She looked sad. Video calling with Dad does that to her sometimes. Nobody talked. I guess we were all lost in our own thoughts.

CHAPTER SIXTEEN

I WOKE WITH A start on the family room floor. The house had that late-night hush. I looked at the clock: ten-thirty. On the couch, Olive snored softly. And Ben . . .

Oh, geez, he wasn't in the easy chair!

I scrambled to my feet.

Not again.

The house was dark except for the glow seeping out from under Mom's studio door and the circle of light from the overhead lamp in the kitchen. Phew! Ben sat beneath it at the table. I sighed with relief. He'd opened the window to catch the night breezes, and was now writing something. He looked so sad and serious as he scrawled

away with that feather and chocolate pudding that I didn't have the heart to tell him about the invention of the ballpoint pen.

"Whatever happened to 'early to bed, early to rise'?" I asked, sitting down next to him.

He looked up with the barest of smiles.

"That was before the invention of the electrical light." He blew on his paper, I guess to help dry the pudding. "I am writing a letter to William."

He read the first lines:

Dearest William,

Can a father turn from his son? He cannot. He should not. I have wronged you, William. Wronged you because I felt you'd wronged me. But, as a wise lad recently reminded me, "two wrongs can never make a right."

"That's nice," I said.

He set down his quill. "I have discovered many marvels during this extraordinary day, Nolan. But methinks *this* was the most marvelous of them all."

We sat at the table in the ring of light, listening to the silence. Ben wore a sad smile, but his eyes were bright. He picked up his quill again and poised it over the paper.

Just then, the calm was broken by a white

glow. Beside him on the kitchen table, the stone in the center of the crystal radio began to radiate light. White . . . whiter . . . crystal white.

Startled, Ben pushed away from the table as scratchy static came through the headphones. "Nolan, your device seems to be functioning again."

I looked at Ben curiously.

The static in the headphones grew louder. First, random pops and crackles. Then the noise seemed to form words. Through the static, I thought I heard the word "home."

"What's happening?" asked Olive. She

stumbled sleepily into the kitchen, rubbing her eyes.

The glow from the crystal radio shone on her face.

"Oh, my gosh, is it on?" Her eyes widened. "It's on!"

We gathered around the radio, staring down stupidly.

It was Olive who finally sprang into action. "Why are we just standing here? We have to send Ben home. Quick, before that thing turns itself off again."

She didn't have to say it twice.

Snatching up his letter, Ben hurried to his place in the doorway.

I put on the headphones.

And Olive reached for the dial. Then—

"Wait!" she cried. She dashed into the family room.

The headphones grew louder, the static more insistent, the word "home" repeated over and over in the whirl of sound.

Ben and I looked at each other.

"Hurry up!" I cried.

Ben looked worried.

At last, she raced back. She was holding the toy fire hat in her hand. "You can't forget this," she said. She shoved it at him and reached for the dial.

"Bye, Benny," she called.

"Good-bye, Ben," I said.

"I shall always remember you, dear children," said Ben, his voice already garbled and sputtering with static.

Click . . . click . . . click.

The world dissolved, the room once again melting into a blur. Then . . .

POP!

The room seemed to snap back like a rubber band and returned to focus.

And Ben was gone.

We stared at the empty space for what seemed like forever. I thought about Ben spinning through time to Philadelphia. "I hope he got home all right."

"He did," said Olive. She pulled out a piece of paper. "I printed this out when I was on the computer. After I talked to Daddy."

It was a picture from E-Cylopedia—
a painting of Ben proudly wearing his toy
fire hat.

I grinned. He looked dorky in *two* centuries. And I realized why Olive insisted he
take the hat. So we'd have proof. So we'd
know he'd gotten home safe.

I looked at the radio. Once again, it had
gone dark and silent.

I stated the obvious. "This is our secret,
Olive. We can't tell anyone about the radio."

Olive nodded slowly. "You don't have to
tell me that."

"Just you and me, Olive," I said.

"No kidding," she said.

"And never mess around with it again."

"Never?" Olive frowned. "That's no fun."

Outside the window, a twig snapped.

Olive and I looked at each other.

"We should have kissed him harder," she said.

I thought of the electrostatic machine sitting in the garage, where we'd parked the wagon. "Forget it," I said.

"Party pooper," grumbled Olive.

And I hollered through the closed curtains, "Good night, Tommy."

The only answer was the soft pat of footsteps moving away.

With a relieved sigh, I reached over and closed the radio's lid. I felt the gold block letters that read PROPERTY OF H.H. It made my fingers tingle.

"Maybe 'H.H.' stands for 'home is where the heart is,'" she said seriously.

I laughed. And suddenly, I thought I understood why the radio had activated; why at that very moment it had come back to life. I repeated what my teacher, Mr. Druff, had said last year: "We learn from the past how to live in the present." Then I grinned and added, "*And* vice versa."

I was still thinking about it all as I carried the radio into my bedroom.

"Don't play with it without me," said Olive from her doorway.

"I told you. We're not playing with it ever again."

"You're not going to throw it away, are you?"

I shook my head. "It was sent to me for a reason, and I have to find out what that reason is. But I'll put it away so no one can touch it. Got it?"

Just in case, I hid the radio deep in my closet, buried in a box of building blocks. So many strange things had happened. It would take a while to figure them out.

I yawned. I'd never felt so tired. But there was one more thing I needed to do before I could sleep. I glanced at the bedside clock. It was morning in London. Plucking my laptop off my desk, I tapped some keys.

"Nolan?"

"Hi, Dad," I said.

EPILOGUE

"COME ON, NOLAN. WE'RE going to be late to my party." Olive careened into my bedroom, wearing a pink sequined mermaid princess Aquamarina bathing suit. On her back flashed a brand-new Shimmer and Sparkle backpack. Both were birthday presents from Dad.

"You'll be the best-dressed mermaid at your pool party," he said when we all video chatted last night.

"And the only one who can scull and flutter," added Olive.

I have to admit, she was pretty excited about her birthday. "Pizza, cake, and mermaid swimming," she had told Mom to write on the invitations.

"Mermaid swimming?" Mom had asked.

"It's a long story," I'd said.

Mom was smiling a lot these days, now that her book—*Bun Franklin and the Pursuit of Hoppiness*—was done. Her editor was even calling it a "sunny, funny, punny, bunny masterpiece."

I finished tying my shoes. "I'm ready, already."

POP!

A bright light shot out from under my closet door. It grew white . . . whiter . . . crystal white. From within its depths came the sounds of static and faint voices. "This is no ordinary . . . *khhhhh* . . . time . . . *khhhhh* . . . You must do . . . *khhhhh* . . . the thing you think you cannot do. . . ."

"It's Ben!" whooped Olive. "He's come back for my birthday!"

She raced to the closet.

"Wait, Olive . . ."

She flung open the door.

And screamed.

And slammed the door shut again. Pressing her back against it, she stretched her arms wide. "That," she panted, "is definitely *not* Ben Franklin."

"Hulloooo!" came a woman's quavering voice. "FD? Is that you? Let me out, won't you? I seem to have gotten trapped in the closet."

A few days after Ben went home, I stopped by the library. I wanted to check out a couple of Captain Blood graphic novels. I also wanted to check out Ben's stories and see if they were true. Not that I thought he was lying or anything, but come on ... *stunt swimming?* With a little help from Mrs. Bustamante, here's what I found out:

STORY #1: BEN AND ELECTRICITY

Back in Ben's day, no one understood what electricity was or what it could do. Ben's experiments were all about trying to figure out electricity's mysteries. And while he went about it pretty scientifically—setting up careful experiments, observing closely, and writing down every step—he liked to have fun, too. Like one time, he made a fake spider. It had a cork for its body and six pieces of thread for its legs, and was attached to a thin wire. When people visited his laboratory, he liked to prank them by electrifying the wire. This made the spider jump and wiggle across his worktable. While people screamed, Ben giggled.

Shocking!

He did other cool stuff with electricity. He made brass balls glow red, produced bolts of lightning, and made his ring of gray hair stand on end. He liked showing off. Sometimes too much, because he really did almost electrocute himself that time he tried to cook a turkey. Lucky for him, he escaped with just a couple of bruises.

Which goes to show how dangerous it was to experiment with electricity. Probably the bravest or stupidest experiment he ever did—depending on how you look at it—was flying a kite in the middle of a thunderstorm. He wanted to prove that lightning was electricity. So he asked his son William to run back and forth across a field in the rain until the kite took flight. Then Ben, who had been standing all dry and cozy in a farmer's shed, took over. Minutes later, he touched his knuckle to a brass key tied to the end of the kite's string and got a shock. His hypothesis was true! And he became famous. The Royal Society of London—sort of a club of the best-of-the-best scientists in Europe—gave him their biggest award, called the Copley Medal. Universities like Harvard and Yale gave him honorary degrees. And the king of France sent him a letter of congratulations.

STORY #2: BEN AND THE FIRST LIBRARY

Ben really did start a club in 1727 that he called . . .

The Gentlemen's Society for the Wearing of Fur Caps? The Mini Mermaid Club for Beginning Mermaids?

. . . the Junto. Every Friday night, he and nine of his smartest friends got together at a tavern to talk about books and politics and ways they could improve their city. Word got around about the club. Other people begged to join.

But Ben wanted to keep each club small—no bigger than twelve members. So he suggested that others form their own clubs. Soon Philadelphia had six groups, all of them dedicated to smart talk and helping the community. They formed Philadelphia's fire department.

I hope they didn't let Ben drive.

And just like Ben said, they established the first library. It's true. It was his idea. And club members did go around collecting money for it. In just a couple of years the library had more than three hundred books and was open from two to three on Wednesday afternoons, and from ten until four on Saturdays. Only people who paid to use the library could check out the books, one at a time, but anyone could go inside and read.

Some of the original books from the first library are still around. You can see them at the Library Company of Philadelphia.

Library Company?

I know—it's a weird name for a library. But that's what Ben called it, and that's what it's still called.

STORY #3: BEN AND SWIM FINS

In Ben's time, hardly anyone knew how to swim. But Ben loved the water, and he taught himself when he was just seven years old. By reading a book called *The Art of Swimming,* he learned how to dive, how to swim holding one foot, and even how to clip his nails underwater.

Ben *did* invent swim fins when he was eleven years old. They were his very first invention, but they weren't his last. During his lifetime he invented all kinds of cool and useful things like bifocals, the odometer, the Franklin stove, the library chair, the glass armonica . . .

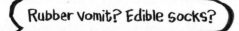
Rubber vomit? Edible socks?

. . . daylight saving time, and a phonic alphabet. And he kept on swimming.

STORY #4: BEN AND WILLIAM

Ben had three kids—Frances Folger (called Franky) born in 1732; Sarah (known as Sally) born in 1743; and his oldest son, William, born in late 1730 or early 1731. Ben and William were very close, especially after little Franky died of smallpox. William went to the best schools, and his books and toys were specially ordered from London. He even had his own pony.

> Yankee Doodle went to town, a-riding on a pony!

Ben and William did everything together. So of course when Ben traveled to London in 1757, William went with him. William was twenty-six by then, and he met the richest, most powerful men in England. Ben was happy about it. He wanted King George III to appoint William as royal Governor of New Jersey. And in 1763 the king did!

William took his job and all of its responsibilities seriously. Even when his father and others began grumbling about how badly the American colonies were being treated by the British government, William stayed loyal to the king. Then revolution broke out and colonists had to choose a side—fight for independence, or fight for Britain. William thought his father would understand when he stuck by the king. But Ben didn't. He told William how he felt: "Nothing has ever hurt me so much . . . and to find myself deserted in my old age by my own son."

Poor Ben.

William felt deserted, too. Colonists eventually arrested William for being an enemy of the country and threw him in jail. Ben could have gotten him out, seeing as how he was a member of the Continental Congress. He'd even been on the committee that wrote the Declaration of Independence. But Ben let William sit in a cell for two whole years. When he was finally released, William moved to London. His dad didn't even say good-bye.

Poor William.

The two didn't meet again until July 1785. The revolution was over, and Ben—who'd been a diplomat in France for the past nine years—was sailing home to Philadelphia. When his ship made a stop in England, William hurried to meet it. He couldn't wait to see his dad. He wanted to be close again.

Oooh, I love happy endings!

But it didn't work out that way. William felt awkward and uncomfortable. Ben was still boiling mad. Two days later, when Ben sailed for America, they still hadn't made up. They never saw each other again.

Wahhhh, I hate sad endings!

William *did* write to him, but I don't think Ben wrote back. If so, he didn't mail the letter. William never heard another word from him.

So that's it. Every last thing Ben told us was true. I guess honesty *is* the best policy.

Here's a list of the books I used to fact-check Ben, otherwise known as my:

BIBLIOGRAPHY

Barretta, Gene. *Now & Ben: The Modern Inventions of Ben Franklin.* New York: Square Fish, 2008.

Byrd, Robert. *Electric Ben: The Amazing Life and Times of Benjamin Franklin.* New York: Dial, 2012.

Fleming, Candace. *Ben Franklin's Almanac: Being a True Account of the Good Gentleman's Life.* New York: Atheneum, 2003.

Giblin, James Cross. *The Amazing Life of Benjamin Franklin.* New York: Scholastic Press, 2006.

Krull, Kathleen. *Benjamin Franklin (Giants of Science).* New York: Puffin Books, 2014.

Olson, Kay Melchisedech. *Benjamin Franklin: An American Genius.* North Mankato, MN: Capstone Press, 2006.

Rockliff, Mara. *Mesmerized: How Benjamin Franklin Solved a Mystery that Baffled All of France.* Somerville, MA: Candlewick, 2015.

Mr. Druff would be impressed, huh?

There are a gazillion websites about Ben, but these two are my favorites:

pbs.org/benfranklin

This has a super-fun Explore section, where you can visit Ben's hometown, or travel with him around the world, or learn to make a kite based on his design. Best of all, there's an interactive electrical experience. You can make a spark, build a lightning rod, or fly a kite in a thunderstorm.

ushistory.org/franklin/info

There's a pretty good biography on this website, as well as essays and stories and a list of Ben quotations. What I liked most, though, were the games, puzzles, and experiments. I even played checkers with Ben . . . and won!

CANDACE FLEMING is the author of the funny middle-grade novels *The Fabled Fourth Graders of Aesop Elementary* and *The Fabled Fifth Graders of Aesop Elementary,* as well as the incredibly interesting nonfiction books *The Great and Only Barnum,* about showman P. T. Barnum, and *Amelia Lost,* about the aviatrix Amelia Earhart. She also wrote a biography about Ben Franklin called *Ben Franklin's Almanac.* She loves Ben so much that, on his 296th birthday on January 17, she baked him a cake. Her sons refused to sing "Happy Birthday" to a "dead guy," so Candace ended up singing by herself. Like Nolan and Olive, Candace lives in Illinois, but you can visit her on the Web at candacefleming.com.

MARK FEARING always thought Ben Franklin would have made a great president. In fact, on a test in third grade, he may have said Ben Franklin *was* a president. Mistakes happen. Mark has illustrated more than a dozen picture books, including *Chicken Story Time* by Sandy Asher and *Three Little Aliens and the Big Bad Robot* by Margaret McNamara, and has written and illustrated cool graphic novels, including *Earthling!* He lives with his wife, daughter, and dog in Oregon—which wasn't even a state when Ben Franklin was alive. Visit Mark on the Web at markfearing.com.